# THE STRONG SHALL LIVE

# THE
# STRONG SHALL
# LIVE

## LOUIS L'AMOUR

BANTAM BOOKS
TORONTO · NEW YORK · LONDON · SYDNEY

To Jackson and Mary Jane . . .

# CONTENTS

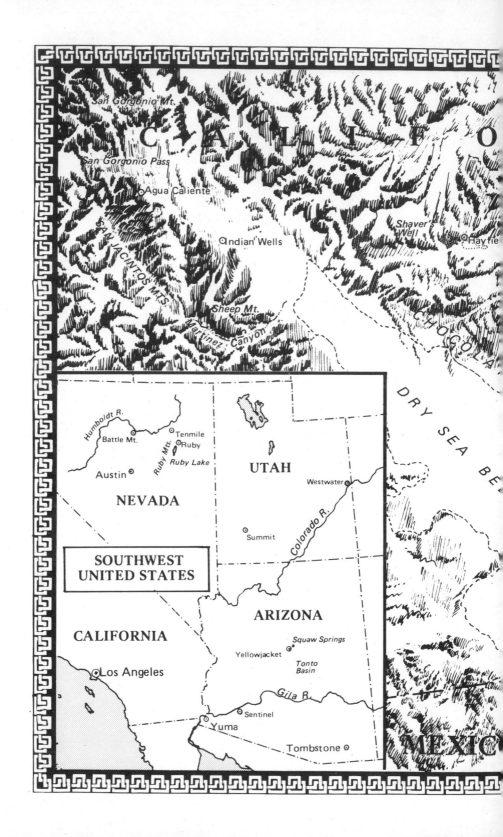

Chuckawalla

Colorado River

ARIZONA

springs

CKA·WALLA MTS.

vation

ass

Chuckawalla
Spring

Little Chuckawalla Mts.

Red Butte Spr.

rock

tanks

Wash

MOUNTAINS

sea level

MOUNTAINS

CHOCOLATE

Alcolita Valley

Algodones (dunes)

Gila River

Yuma

TINAJAS ALTAS

**CHOCOLATE MOUNTAINS
CALIFORNIA**

Miles

0   5   10   15   20   25   30

Map by Alan McKnight

# FOREWORD

This book is a partial answer to those readers who have been asking where my short stories could be found. A previous collection appeared as WAR PARTY, and now these.

A few of the stories were written long ago, others quite recently. All are, I believe, illustrative of the title of the collection.

Not long ago a writer, attempting to find a progression in the development of my stories according to a pattern of his own devising, predicted that soon I would write a story with an ethnic hero. He was over thirty years late. Merrano, in this volume, is one such case, although there were others.

My stories have nothing to do with race, creed, or nationality. They are simply stories of people on the frontier, and those people were of all kinds. If sometimes they resemble one another it is simply a pattern imposed upon them by the country and the time.

The frontier was itself selective. It tended to eliminate the weak and the inefficient by one means or another.

In these stories there are no "heroes" in the usual sense,

*although in the Homeric sense there may be. These are stories of people living out their lives against a background that demanded all they could give and often a bit more. They were people trying to find acceptable patterns of behavior in a totally new environment, drawing upon their past but adjusting themselves to new situations and attitudes.*

*The frontier demanded they be self-reliant. Group-thinking and peer behavior had only a limited application.*

*The West has been portrayed as lawless. This is literally untrue. The pioneers brought their church, their schools, and their town meetings with them. Necessarily, there were alterations in the laws they established to conform with changed conditions, but the law was there. It is true there were many free spirits who resented this, and there were others who came west intending to do as they pleased. The existence of Boot Hills in many western towns is ample evidence of how the frontier coped with such problems.*

*It had been the custom of men, from the beginning of time, to settle disputes by combat. From the club and spear, men progressed to the lance and the sword and then to the pistol. Senators, cabinet officers, admirals, and generals regularly settled their disputes with weapons. There were undoubtedly as many duels in the early American Navy as in any region of the West. Stephen Decatur, one of our early naval heroes, killed as many men in duels as did Bat Masterson, who, incidentally, wound up his days as a sportswriter on a New York newspaper, and died not with a pistol in his hands, but a typewriter.*

*—Louis L'Amour*

# THE STRONG SHALL LIVE

The land was fire beneath and the sky was brass above, but throughout the day's long riding the bound man sat erect in the saddle and cursed them for thieves and cowards. Their blows did not silence him, although the blood from his swollen and cracked lips had dried on his face and neck.

Only John Sutton knew where they rode and only he knew what he planned for Cavagan, and John Sutton sat thin and dry and tall on his long-limbed horse, leading the way.

Nine men in all, tempered to the hard ways of an unforgiving land, men strong in the strengths needed to survive in a land that held no place for the weak or indecisive. Eight men and a prisoner taken after a bitter chase from the pleasant coastal lands to the blazing desert along the Colorado River.

Cavagan had fought on when the others quit. They destroyed his crops, tore down his fences, and burned his home. They killed his hired hand and tried to kill him. When they burned his home he rebuilt it, and when they shot at him he shot back.

1

When they ambushed him and left him for dead, he crawled into the rocks like a wounded grizzly, treated his own wounds, and then caught a horse and rode down to Sutton's Ranch and shot out their lights during the victory celebration.

Two of Sutton's men quit in protest, for they admired a game man, and Cavagan was winning sympathy around the country.

Cavagan was a black Irishman from County Sligo. His mother died on the Atlantic crossing and his father was killed by Indians in Tennessee. At sixteen Cavagan fought in the Texas war for independence, trapped in the Rockies for two years, and in the war with Mexico he served with the Texas Rangers and learned the value of a Walker Colt.

At thirty he was a man honed by desert fires and edged by combat with fist, skull, and pistol. Back in County Sligo the name had been O'Cavagan and the family had a reputation won in battle.

Sutton's men surrounded his house a second time thinking to catch him asleep. They fired at the house and waited for him to come out. Cavagan had slept on the steep hillside behind the house and from there he opened fire, shooting a man from his saddle and cutting the lobe from Sutton's ear with a bullet intended to kill.

Now they had him, but he sat straight in the saddle and cursed them. Sutton he cursed but he saved a bit for Beef Hannon, the Sutton foreman.

"You're a big man, Beef," he taunted, "but untie my hands and I'll pound that thick skull of yours until the yellow runs out of your ears."

Their eyes squinted against the white glare and the blistering heat from off the dunes, and they tried to ignore him. Among the sand dunes there was no breeze, only the stifling heaviness of hot, motionless air. Wearily their horses plodded along the edge of a dune where the sand fell steeply off into a deep pit among the dunes. John Sutton drew rein. "Untie his feet," he said.

Juan Velasquez swung down and removed the rawhide thongs from Cavagan's feet, and then stood back, for he knew the manner of man that was Cavagan.

"Get down," Sutton told Cavagan.

Cavagan stared his contempt from the slits where his eyes peered through swollen, blackened flesh, then he swung his leg across the saddle, kicked his boot free of the stirrup and dropped to the ground.

Sutton regarded him for several minutes, savoring his triumph, then he put the flat of his boot against Cavagan's back and pushed. Cavagan staggered, fought for balance, but the sand crumbled beneath him and he fell, tumbling to the bottom of the hollow among the dunes.

With his hands tied and his body stiff from the beatings he had taken he needed several minutes to get to his feet. When he stood erect he stared up at Sutton. "It is what I would have expected from you," he said.

Sutton's features stiffened, and he grew white around the mouth. "You're said to be a tough man, Cavagan. I've heard it until I'm sick of it, so I've brought you here to see how much is tough and how much is shanty Irish bluff. I am curious to see how tough you will be without food or water. We're leaving you here."

Hannon started to protest. He had himself tried to kill Cavagan, but to leave a man to die in the blazing heat of the desert without food or water and with his hands bound . . . a glance at Sutton's face and the words died on his lips.

"It's sixty miles to water," he managed, at last.

John Sutton turned in his saddle and measured Hannon with a glance, then deliberately he faced front and started away. Reluctantly, the others followed.

Juan Velasquez looked down into the pit at Cavagan. He carried a raw wound in his side from a Cavagan bullet, but that pit was seventy feet deep. Slowly, thinking as he did it, Juan unfastened his canteen and was about to toss it to Cavagan when he caught Sutton's eyes on him.

"Throw it," Sutton suggested, "but if you do you will follow it."

Juan balanced the canteen on his palm, tempted beyond measure. Sixty miles? With the temperature at one hundred and twenty degrees? Reluctantly, he retied the canteen to his saddle horn. Sutton watched him, smiling his thin smile.

"I'll remember that, Juan," Cavagan said. "It was a good thought."

John Sutton turned his square thin shoulders and rode away, the others following. Hannon's shoulders were hunched as if expecting a blow.

When the last of them had disappeared from sight, Cavagan stood alone at the bottom of the sand pit.

This was 1850 and even the Indians avoided the sand hills. There was no law west of Santa Fe or east of the coast mountains. Cavagan had settled on land that Sutton considered his, although he had no legal claim to it. Other would-be settlers had been driven off, but Cavagan would not be driven. To make matters worse he courted the girl Sutton had marked for himself.

Cavagan stood in the bottom of the sand pit, his eyes closed against the glare of the sun on the white sand. He told himself, slowly, harshly, that he would not, he must not die. Aloud he said, *"I shall live! I shall see him die!"*

There was a burning fury within him but a caution born of experience. Shade would come first to the west side of the pit, so with his boot he scraped a small pit in the sand. There, several inches below the surface, it was a little cooler. He sat down, his back to the sun, and waited.

More than seven hours of sunlight remained. To attempt climbing from the pit or even to fight the thongs on his wrists would cause him to perspire profusely and lessen his chances of ultimate survival. From this moment he must be patient, he must think.

Sweat dripped from his chin, his throat was parched and the sun on his back and shoulders was like the heat from a furnace. An hour passed, and then another. When at last he looked up there was an inch of shadow under the western lip of the pit.

He studied the way his wrists were bound. His hands had been tied to the pommel, so they were in front of him. He lifted his wrists to his teeth and began ever so gently to work at the rawhide knots. It took nearly an hour, but by the time his wrists were free the shade had reached the bottom of the pit. He coiled the rawhide and slipped it into his pocket.

The east slope was somewhat less steep, with each step he slid back, but with each he gained a little. Finally he climbed out and stood in the full glare of the setting sun.

He knew where the nearest water hole lay but knew Sutton would have it guarded. His problem was simple. He had to find water, get out of the desert, then find a horse and weapons. He intended to destroy Sutton as he would destroy a rabid wolf.

Shadows stretched out from the mountains. To the north the myriad pinnacles of the Chocolate Mountains crowned themselves with gold from the setting sun. He started to walk.

It was not sixty miles to the nearest water, for Cavagan knew the desert better than Sutton. West of him, but in a direction he dare not chance, lay Sunset Spring. Brackish water, and off the line for him.

Twenty-five miles to the northwest among the pinnacles of the Chocolates were rock tanks that might contain water. A Cahuilla Indian had told him of the natural reservoir, and upon this feeble chance he rested his life.

He walked northwest, his chances a thousand to one. He must walk only in the early hours of the morning and after sundown. During the day he must lie in the shade, if he found any, and wait. To walk in the sun without water was to die.

The sand was heavy and at each step he sank to his ankles. Choosing a distant peak in the Chocolates he pointed himself toward it. When the stars came out he would choose a star above it for a guide. At night landmarks have a way of losing themselves and what was familiar by day becomes strange and unfamiliar in the darkness.

To reach the vicinity of the rock tanks was one thing, to find them quite another. Near such tanks in the Tinajas Altas men had died of thirst within a few feet of water, unaware of its presence. Such tanks were natural receptacles catching the runoff from infrequent rains, and so shaded, that evaporation was slow. As there was no seepage there was no vegetation to indicate the presence of water.

The shadows grew long and only a faint afterglow remained in the sky. On his right and before him lay the valley dividing the dunes from the Chocolate Mountains. Now the air was cool and here and there a star appeared. Desert air is thin and does not retain the heat, hence it soon becomes cool, and in the middle of the night, actually cold. These were the hours Cavagan must use.

If he could not find the tanks, or if there was no water in them, he would die. Cavagan was a man without illusion. His great strength had been sapped by brutal treatment, and he must conserve what strength remained. Locating his peak and a star above it, he walked on. A long time later, descending from the last of the dunes, he took a diagonal course across the valley. Twice he paused to rest, soaking up the coolness. He put a small pebble in his mouth to start the saliva flowing. For a time it helped.

Walking in heavy sand he had made but two miles an hour, but on the valley floor he moved faster. If he reached the *tinajas* and they held water he would have achieved one goal. However, he had no way of carrying water and the next water hole was far. Not that one can place reliance on any desert water hole. Often they were used up or had gone dry.

His battered face throbbed with every step and his head ached. The pinnacles of the Chocolates loomed nearer, but he was not deceived. They were miles away.

An hour before dawn he entered a wash that came down from the Chocolates. He was dead tired, and his feet moved awkwardly. In eleven hours he had probably traveled no more than twenty-three or -four miles and should be near the tanks. He found a ledge that offered shade and stretched out. He was soon asleep.

The heat awakened him. His mouth was dry as parchment and he had difficulty in moving his tongue, which seemed awkward and swollen. A glance at the sun told him it was noon or nearly so. According to the Cahuilla he should be within a few yards of water, certainly within a mile or so. In that maze of cliffs, boulders, rock slabs, and arroyos, cluttered with canelike clumps of ocotillo, he would be fortunate to find anything.

Animals would come to water but many desert creatures lived without it, getting what moisture they needed from succulent plants or cacti. Some insects sought water, and he had noticed bees flying past taking the straight line that usually led to hive or water.

His throat was raw and his mind wandered. Far off, over the desert he had recently crossed, lay a lovely blue lake, shimmering among the heat waves . . . a mirage.

Lying down again he waited for dusk. He was sweating no longer and movement was an effort. He had been almost thirty hours without water and in intense heat.

It was almost dark when he awakened again. Staggering to his feet he started to climb. The coolness refreshed him and gave him new strength. He pushed on, climbing higher. His vision was uncertain and his skull throbbed painfully, but at times he felt an almost delirious gaiety, and then he would scramble up rocks with zest and abandon. Suddenly he sat down. With a shock of piercing clarity he realized he could die.

He rarely thought of dying, although he knew it was expected of him as of all men, yet it was always somebody else who was dying. Suddenly he realized he had no special dispensation against death and he could die now, within the hour.

It was faintly gray in the east when he started again. Amazingly, he found the tanks.

A sheep track directed him. It was a half-sheltered rock tank, but it was dry. Only a faint dusting of sand lay in the bottom.

A few minutes later, and a little higher up, he found a second tank. It was bone-dry.

Soon the sun would rise and the heat would return. Cavagan stared at the empty tanks and tried to swallow, but could not. His throat was raw, and where it was not raw it felt like old rubber. His legs started to tremble, but he refused to sit down. He knew if he sat now he might never get up. There was a queerness in him, a strange lightness as if he no longer possessed weight. Through the semi-delirium induced by heat, thirst, and exhaustion there remained a hard core of resolution, the firmness of a course resolved upon and incomplete. If he quit now John Sutton would have won. If he quit now the desert would have defeated him, and the desert was a friendly place to those who knew how to live with it.

Cunning came to him. To those who knew how to live *with* it, not against it. No man could fight the desert and live. A man must move with it, give with it, live by its rules. He had done that, so what remained?

His eyes peered into the growing light, refusing to focus properly, his thoughts prowling the foggy lowlands of his mind, seeking some forgotten thing.

Think back . . . the rock tanks of the Chocolates. The Chocolates. The Chocolates were a range running parallel to the dunes which the Mexicans called the *algodones*. Bit by bit his thoughts tried to sort out something he knew, but something was missing. Something else the Cahuilla had said. It came to him then like the Indian's voice in his ears. *"If there is no water in the tanks, there is a seep in the canyon."*

Almost due west was the canyon through which ran the old Indian trail . . . maybe five miles.

It was too far. And then he got up without decision and walked away. He walked with his head up, his mind gone off somewhere, walking with a quick, lively step. When he had walked for some distance he fell flat on his face.

A lizard on a rock stared at him, throat throbbing. Something stirred Cavagan's muscles, and he got his hands under him and pushed himself to his knees. Then he got up, weaving a little. It was daylight.

A bee flew past.

He swayed a little, brow puckered, a bee flying straight . . . hive or water or a hive near water? He took a few hesitant steps in the direction the bee had flown, then stopped. After a bit another droned past and he followed, taking a sight on a clump of ocotillo some distance off. He stumbled and fell, scarcely conscious of it until he arose and stared at his palms, lacerated by the sharp gravel.

When he fell again he lay still for what must have been a considerable time, finally becoming aware of a whistling sound. He pushed himself up, listening. The sound reminded him of a cricket, yet was not a cricket. He listened, puzzled yet alerted for some reason he did not understand.

He moved then, and under a clump of greasewood something stirred. He froze, thinking first of a rattler, although the heat was too great for one to be out unless in a well-shaded position. And then his eye caught a movement, and he knew why the sound had alerted him. It was a tiny red-spotted toad.

Long ago he had learned that the red-spotted toad always lived within the vicinity of water and never got far from it.

Awkwardly he got to his feet and looked carefully around. His eyes could not seem to focus properly, yet down the canyon he glimpsed some galleta grass and walked toward it, coming upon the seep quite suddenly.

Dropping to his knees he scooped water in his palm and drank it. A cold trickle down his throat was painful on the raw flesh. With gentle fingers he put water on his lips, bathed his cheeks and face with it, then drank a little more.

Something inside was crying out that he was safe, but he knew he was not. He drank a little more, then crawled into the shade of a rock and lay on his back and slept.

When he awakened he crawled out and drank more and more, his water-starved body soaking up the moisture. He had found water but had no means of carrying it with him, and the canyon of the seep might well become his tomb, his open tomb.

Cavagan got out the rawhide with which his wrists had been bound and rigged a snare for small game. In placing the snare he found some seeds, which he ate. He drank again, then sat down to think his way forward.

From where he now sat there were two possible routes. Northeast toward the Colorado was Red Butte Spring, but it was at least twenty-five miles away and in the wrong direction.

The twelve miles to Chuckawalla Spring began to loom very large, and leaving the water he had found worried him. The Chuckawalla Mountains were a thin blue line on the northern horizon, and even if he reached them the next spring beyond was Corn Springs, just as far away. Yet the longer he waited the more his strength would be drained by lack of food. He had never known such exhaustion, yet he dare not wait.

On the second morning his snare caught a kangaroo rat, which he broiled over a small fire. When he had eaten he got up abruptly, drank some more, glanced at the notch in the Chuckawallas and started walking.

At the end of an hour he rested, then went on at a slower pace. The heat was increasing. In midafternoon he fell on his face and did not get up.

More than an hour must have passed before he became aware of the intense heat and began to crawl like a blind mole, seeking shade. The plants about him were less than a foot high, and he found nothing, finally losing consciousness.

He awakened, shaking with chill. The moon cast a ghostly radiance over the desert, the clustered canes of the ocotillo looking like the headdresses of gigantic Indians. He got to his feet, aware of a stirring in the night. He waited, listening. A faint click of a hoof on stone and then he saw a desert bighorn sheep walk into the wash and then he heard a faint splash. Rising, he walked down to the wash and heard a scurry of movement as the sheep fled. He almost walked into the spring before he saw it. He drank, then drank again.

Late the next afternoon he killed a chuckawalla with a well-thrown stone. He cooked the big lizard and found the meat tender and appetizing. At dusk he started again, crossing a small saddle to the north side of the mountains. It was twelve miles this time, and it was daybreak before he reached Corn Springs. He recognized it by the clump of palms and mesquite in the wash before reaching the spring, some clumps of *baccharis*, clusters of small twigs rising two to three feet. And then he found the spring itself. After drinking he crawled into the shade and was asleep almost at once.

He opened his eyes, aware of wood-smoke. Rolling over quickly, he sat up.

An old man squatted near a kettle at a fire near the spring, and on the slope a couple of burros browsed.

"Looks to me like you've had a time of it," the old man commented. "You et anything?"

"Chuckawalla . . . had a kangaroo rat a couple of days ago."

The old man nodded. "Et chuck a time or two . . . ain't as bad as some folks might figger."

Cavagan accepted a bowl of stew and ate slowly, savoring every bite. Finally, placing the half-empty bowl on the ground he sat back. "Don't suppose a man with a pipe would have a cigarette paper?"

"You started that Mex way of smokin'? Ain't for it, m'self. Give me a pipe ever' time." The old man handed him his tobacco pouch and dug into his duffle for a rolled up newspaper. "Don't tear the readin' if you can he'p. A body don't find much readin' in the desert and sometimes I read through a newspaper five or six times."

Cavagan wiped his fingers on his pants and rolled a smoke with trembling fingers. Then he put the cigarette down and ate a few more bites before lighting up.

"Come far?"

"Fifty-five, sixty miles."

"An' no canteen? You had yourself a time." The old man said his name was Pearson. He volunteered no more than that. Nor did he ask questions. There were not four white men between the San Jacintos and the Colorado River.

"I've got to get to that hot spring this side of the pass, up there by the San Jacintos," Cavagan said. "I can get a horse from the Cahuillas."

The old man stirred his fire and moved the coffeepot closer. "You listen to me you won't go back."

"You know who I am?"

"Got no idea. Figgered you didn't get where you was by chance. Six years I been prospectin' hereabouts an' I ain't seen nobody but a Chemehuevi or a Cahuilla in this here country. A man would have himself an outfit, gun, knife, canteen. Strikes me somebody left you out here apurpose."

"If you could let me have a canteen or a water sack. Maybe a knife."

"How d' you figger to get out of here?"

"West to the Hayfields, then Shaver's Well and the Yuma stage road."

Pearson studied him out of shrewd old eyes. "You ain't no pilgrim. You made it this far on nerve an' savvy, so mayhap you'll go all the way."

He tamped his pipe. "Tell you something. You fight shy of them Hayfields. Seen a couple of gents settin' on that water with rifles. A body could figger they was waitin' for somebody."

The old man helped Cavagan to more stew. He rarely looked directly at Cavagan.

"Are they on the Hayfields or back up the draw?"

Pearson chuckled. "You do know this country. They're on the Hayfields, an' could be they don't know the source of that water. Could be you're figurin' a man might slip around them, get water, and nobody the wiser."

"If a man had a water sack he might get as far as Hidden Spring."

The old man looked up sharply. "Hidden Spring? Never heard of it."

"Southwest of Shaver's . . . maybe three miles. Better water than Shaver's."

"You must be Cavagan."

Cavagan did not reply. He finished the stew, rinsed the bowl, then filled his coffee cup.

"Nobody knows this country like Cavagan. That's what they say. Nobody can ride as far or shoot as straight as Cavagan. They say that, too. They also say Cavagan is dead, left in the *algodones* with his hands tied. Lots of folks set store by Cavagan. Them Californios, they like him."

Cavagan slept the day away, and the night following. Pearson made no move to leave, but loafed about. Several times he cooked, and he watched Cavagan eat.

Cavagan found him studying some Indian writing. "Can't make head nor tail of it," Pearson complained. "If them Cahuillas can, they won't say."

"This was done by the Old Ones," Cavagan said, "the People Who Went Before. I've followed their trails in the mountains and across the desert."

"They left trails?"

"A man can go from here to the Cahuilla village at Martinez.

The trail follows the canyon back of the village and goes back of Sheep Mountain. There's a branch comes down back of Indian Wells and another goes to the Indian village at the hot spring at the entrance to San Gorgonio Pass. There's a way over the mountains to the coast, too."

Back beside the fire Cavagan added coffee to what was in the pot, then more water before putting it on the fire. Pearson watched him. "Met a damn fool once who throwed out the grounds . . . throwed away the mother. Never seen the like. Can't make proper coffee until she's two, three days old."

He lit his pipe. "A man like you, he might know a lot about water holes. Worth a lot to a man, knowin' things like that."

"The rock tanks in the Chocolates are dry this year," Cavagan said, "but there's a seep in Salvation Pass." He poked twigs under the coffeepot. "Twenty, twenty-two miles east of Chuckawalla there's a red finger of butte. Maybe a quarter of a mile east of that butte there's a little canyon with a seep of water comin' out of the rock. Good water."

"Place like that could save a man's life," Pearson commented. "Good to know things like that."

"The Cahuillas used the old trails. They know the springs."

Wind was rustling the dry palm leaves when Cavagan crawled out in the early dawn and stirred the coals to life to make coffee.

Pearson shook out his boots, then put on his hat. When he had his boots on he went to the limb where his pants were hung and shook them out. A scorpion about four inches long dropped from a trouser leg and scampered away.

"Last time it was a sidewinder in my boot. A body better shake out his clothes before he puts 'em on."

Pearson slipped suspenders over his shoulders. "Figger you'll hit the trail today. If you rustle through that stuff of mine you'll find you a water sack. Crossin' that ol' sea bottom out there, you'll need it." He hitched his shoulders to settle his suspenders. "Still find shells along that ol' beach."

"Cahuillas say a ship came in here once, a long time ago."

"If they say it," Pearson said, "it did."

Cavagan filled the bag after rinsing it, then dipped it in water from the spring. Evaporation would keep it cool.

Pearson took a long knife from his gear. "Never catered to that one m'self, but a body never knows when he'll need an extry."

Cavagan shouldered the sack and thrust the knife into his belt. "Look me up some time," he said. "Just ask for Cavagan."

Pearson's back was turned, packing gear, when Cavagan spoke. He let him take a dozen steps, and then said, "You get to Los Angeles, you go to the Calle de los Negros. Ask for Jake. He owes me money an' I expect he might have a pistol. Get whatever you need."


John Sutton sat at dinner at one end of a long table in his ranch house at Calabasas. The dinner had been enhanced by a turkey killed the day before at a *cienaga* a few miles away. He was restless, but there was no reason for it. Almost a month had gone by. His men had returned to the *algodones* but found no trace of Cavagan. Nor had they expected to. He would have died out on the desert somewhere.

Juan Velasquez saw the rider come up the canyon as he loafed near the gate, standing guard. At the gate the rider dismounted and their eyes met in the gathering dusk. "Buenos noches, Senor," Juan said. "I had expected you."

"So?"

"I have an uncle in Sonora, Senor. He grows old, and he asks for me."

"Adios, Juan."

"Adios, Senor."

Cavagan walked up the steps and into the house where John Sutton sat at dinner.

# ONE NIGHT STAND

Stephen Malone was tall, handsome, immaculate, and broke. He lay on his back, hands clasped behind his head, trying not to think about breakfast. Three weeks ago he had been playing lead roles in *Hearts of Oak, Hamlet,* and *Davy Crockett* on successive nights. Then the bookings ran out, the play closed, and the manager skipped town with the company funds, leaving them stranded.

For some time he had been aware of voices in the next room. A girl was speaking. "He can't! He wouldn't dare!"

The man's tone was touched with despair. "They say he's killed fourteen men. For the kind of money Mason would pay, the Kid wouldn't hesitate to make it fifteen."

There was a pause. "Even before my hand was crippled I couldn't match him. Now I wouldn't stand a chance."

"But Pa, if Hickok comes—?"

"If he can get here in time! He's not the kind to forget what I did for him, but unless he shows up I'm finished. Else, I'd give

15

a thousand dollars to see Bill Hickok walk through the door right now!"

Stephen Malone knew a cue when he heard one. He stepped into the hall and rapped on the door of their room.

"Who's there?" It was the man's voice.

"Bill Hickok."

The door opened and he was facing a thin old man with gray hair, and a pretty, dark-haired girl. "You aren't Bill Hickok!" The man was disgusted.

"No," Malone said, "but for a thousand dollars I will be."

"You're a gunfighter?" Else demanded.

"I'm an actor. It is my business to make people believe I am somebody else."

"This is different. This isn't playacting."

"He could kill you," Else said. "You wouldn't have a chance."

"Not if I'm a good enough actor. Not many men would try to draw a gun on Wild Bill Hickok."

"It's a fool idea," the man said.

"So there's an element of risk. I've played Hamlet, Macbeth, and Shylock. Why not Wild Bill?"

"Look, son, you've undoubtedly got nerve, and probably you're a fine actor, but this man is a killer. Oh, I know he's a tinhorn, but you wouldn't have a chance!"

"Not if I'm a good enough actor."

"He's talking nonsense, and you both know it!" Else protested.

"To play Hickok, son, you've got to be able to shoot like Hickok."

"Only if I play it badly. You say the Kid is a tinhorn, I'll trust to your judgment and my skill."

Brady walked to the window. "It might work, you know. It just might."

"It would be suicide!" Else objected.

Brady turned from the window. "I am Emmett Brady. This is my daughter, Else. Frank Mason wants my range, and the Pioche Kid is a friend of his. He was brought here to kill me."

"The pleasure will be mine, sir." Malone bowed.

"Did anyone see you come into the hotel?" Brady asked.

"Only the man at the desk. It was two o'clock in the morning."

"Then it's all right. Jim Cooley is a friend of mine."

"Get him to spread the story that Hickok is in town, and once the story is around, I'll make my play."

"It's ridiculous!" Else declared. "Why should you risk your life for us?"

"Miss Brady, as much as I'd enjoy posing as Sir Galahad, I cannot. I'm no knight in armor, just a stranded actor. But for a thousand dollars? I haven't made that much in a whole season!"

"You've got sand, Malone. Else, fetch Jim Cooley."

"You've still time to back out," Else warned.

"I am grateful for your concern but this will be the first time I have been offered one thousand dollars for a single performance."

Returning to his room, Malone opened his trunk and chose a blond wig with hair to his shoulders. He selected a drooping mustache. ". . . And the buckskin jacket I wore as Davy Crockett. Then I'll remove the plume from this hat I wore in *Shenandoah*—"

The Pioche Kid stared complacently into his glass. Brady was an old man with a bad right hand. He was nothing to worry about.

Jim Cooley came through the swinging doors. "Give me a shot, Sam." He glanced around the room. "Wait until you boys hear who is in town! Wild Bill himself! Rode in last night, all the way from Kansas because he heard his old friend Emmett Brady needed help!"

The Pioche Kid went sick with shock. Somebody was asking what Brady had on Hickok. "Nursed him back to health after a gunshot wound. Hickok nearly killed a couple of horses getting here. He's sleeping it off over at the hotel now."

*Wild Bill Hickok!* The Kid hadn't bargained for this. He took up his whiskey and tossed it off, but the shudder that followed was not caused by the whiskey.

"Sam . . . ?" He pushed the empty glass toward him.

He could feel the excitement in the room. They were thinking they'd see the Pioche Kid shoot it out with Wild Bill Hickok, the most famous of them all.

Somebody mentioned the fourteen men the Kid was supposed to have killed, but the Kid himself knew there had been but four, and two of those had been drunken cowhands, and one of them a drunken farmer who had never held a pistol before.

Suddenly, desperately, he wanted out. How had he got into this, anyway? Hickok could *shoot*! He recalled the stories of Hickok's famous target matches with the renowned Major Talbot, at Cheyenne.

"He's the best," Cooley was saying. "Eyes in the back of his head, seems like. Remember the time he killed Phil Coe, then turned and killed a man running up behind him?"

Cooley smiled at the Kid. "Should be something, you and him. You've killed more than he has if you discount those he killed while a sharpshooter in the Army. But I did see him take four at once. Killed two, a third died later, and the fourth was never any good for anything after."

Cooley finished his drink. "I'm gettin' out of here. I've seen too many bystanders get gut-shot. Sorry I can't wish you luck, Kid, but Bill's a friend of mine."

Men moved to the tables, away from the bar. One hastily paid for his drink and left the bar. The Kid was alone, isolated, cut off.

What the hell was happening? This was *Hickok*! If he won they'd all slap him on the back and buy him drinks, but if he lost they'd just stare at the body as they walked by. He mopped his face. He was soaked with sweat, and he knew why. He was scared.

Mason was at the door. "He's comin', Kid. Be something to be known as the man who killed Wild Bill."

Malone paused in the door to wave at someone down the street, then he walked to the bar. All eyes were on him. "Rye, if you please."

Sam put a bottle and a glass before him. The Kid licked dry lips with a fumbling tongue. Desperately he wanted to wipe his palm dry on his pants, but he was afraid Hickok would think he was going for a gun. Now was the time. He should open the ball. Sweat dripped from his face to the bar. He opened his mouth to speak, but Malone spoke first.

"Bartender, I'd like to find two men for a little job. I'll pay a dollar each. It's a digging job."

"You said . . . a *digging* job?"

"That's right. I want two men to dig a hole about—" he turned deliberately and looked right at the Kid, "—six feet long, six feet deep, and three wide."

"Whereabouts do you want it dug?"

"On Boot Hill."

"A grave?"

"Exactly."

Sam motioned to two men at a nearby table. "Tom? Joe? Mr. Hickok wants a couple of men." He hesitated ever so slightly. "To dig a grave."

"And to make a slab for a marker," Malone said.

Sam was loving every moment of it. "You want a name on it?"

"Don't bother with the name. Within the week they will have forgotten who he was, anyway. Just carve on it HE SHOULD HAVE LEFT BEFORE THE SUN WENT DOWN."

He finished his drink. "Good afternoon, gentlemen."

He strolled to the door, paused briefly with his hand on the door, then stepped out on the boardwalk and turned toward the hotel.

Within the saloon a chair creaked as someone shifted weight. The Kid lifted a fumbling hand to brush away the sweat from his face and the hand trembled. He tossed off his drink, spilling a little on his chin. Never had death seemed so close.

What kind of a damned fool was he, anyway? What did he have to do with Brady? Let Mason do his own killing. Suddenly all he wanted was to be away, away from those watching eyes, staring at him, so willing to see him die.

What did he owe Mason? All he had to do was cross the street, mount his horse and ride. Behind his back they would sneer, but what did that matter? He owed these people nothing, and there were a thousand towns like this. Moreover, he'd be alive . . . *alive!*

He wanted to feel the sunshine on his face, the wind in his hair, to drink a long, cold drink of water. He wanted to live!

Abruptly, he walked to the door. He had seen men die, seen them lie tormented in the bloody dust. He did not want to feel the tearing agony of a bullet in his guts.

There was Hickok, his broad back to him, only a few paces away. A quick shot . . . he could always say Hickok had turned.

Sweat dripped into his eyes, dimly he remembered *eyes in the back of his head*. On that other occasion Hickok had turned suddenly and fired . . . dead center.

The Kid let go of his gun as if it were red hot.

Yet he could still make it. He was a pretty good shot . . . well, a fair shot. He could—

Two men emerged from the livery stable, each carrying a shovel. Tom and Joe, to dig a grave . . . *his* grave?

He crossed the street, almost running, and jerked loose the tie-rope. He missed the stirrup with his first try, made it on the second, and was almost crying when he hit the saddle. He wheeled the horse from the hitch-rail and left town at a dead run.

His saddle was hot from the sun, but he could *feel* it. The wind was in his face . . . he was free! He was riding, he was living, and there were a lot of other towns, a lot of country.

Brady turned from the window. "He's gone, Else. Malone did it."

"Mason's leaving, too," she added.

The door opened behind them and Stephen Malone stepped in, removing his hat, then the wig and the mustache. "That's one part I never want to play again!"

"Here's your money, son. You earned it."

"Thanks."

"What would you have done, Malone," Cooley asked, "if the Kid had called your hand?"

"Done? Why this—!"

His draw was surprisingly fast, and he fired at Cooley, point-blank. Cooley sprang back, shocked. His hands clutched his abdomen.

His hands came away and he stared at them. No blood. No—!

Malone was smiling.

"Blanks!" Cooley exclaimed. "You faced the Kid with nothing in your gun but blanks!"

"Well, why not? It was all part of the act."

# TRAIL TO SQUAW SPRINGS

Jim Bostwick was packing a grouch, and he didn't care who knew it. The rain that began with a cloudburst had degenerated into a gullywashing downpour that for forty-eight hours showed no indication of letup. Bostwick, riding a flea-bitten cantankerous roan, was headed for the mountains to file a claim.

Rain slanted dismally across the country before him, pounding on his back and shoulders, beating on the yellow slicker until his back was actually sore. Under a lowering gray sky the rain drew a metallic veil over the country, turning the road into a muddy path across what had been desert two days ago and would be desert again within two hours after the rain ended.

Bostwick swore at the roan who merely twitched his ears, being familiar with cowhands and their ways. He knew the cussing didn't mean anything, and he knew the man who rode him took better care of him than any rider he'd had.

Bostwick swore because he wanted breakfast, wanted a drink,

22

because he hadn't slept the night before, because he needed a shave and his face itched, and he swore on general principles.

His boss on the Slash Five had given him five days off in which to file on his claim, get drunk or whatever he pleased, and it looked like it would rain the whole five days, which Bostwick took as a personal affront.

Bostwick was a cowhand. Not a top hand, just a good, six-days-a-week, fourteen-hours-a-day cowhand who could handle a rope or a branding-iron, dig postholes, mend fences, clean water holes, shoe a horse, and play a fair hand of bunkhouse poker.

He was twenty-nine years old, had never married, and he made forty dollars a month. Several times a month he managed to get good and drunk. And every drunk began or ended with a fistfight. To date he was breaking even on the fights.

He wore a gun but had never drawn it in anger in his life. He had killed only one man he knew of, an Indian who was trying to steal his horse. That was when he was sixteen and coming West in a covered wagon.

At five eleven and weighing one hundred and seventy pounds his method of fighting was simple, to wade in swinging until something hit the dirt, either him or the other fellow. He fought because he enjoyed it and never carried a grudge that lasted longer than the headache.

The rain-blackened lava flow on his left ended and the trail curved around it into a huddle of nondescript buildings, for the most part unpainted and weather-beaten. This was the town of Yellowjacket.

The main street was empty, empty except for a covered wagon whose off wheels were on higher ground, giving a precarious tilt to the wagonbed. A man in a tattered slicker stood before the wagon talking to a girl whose face was barely revealed through the parted canvas.

"He doesn't plan to give them back, Ruthie," the old man was saying. "He doesn't aim to ever give them back. He says we owe him because he fed them."

The thin, querulous voice carried through the rain to Bostwick who turned his eyes to them. There was something about the large dark eyes and the thin child's face that disturbed him. As he drew abreast of them the old man looked up at him out of faded blue eyes, then back to the girl.

"You'd better get into the wagon, Grandad. We can't do anything until the storm breaks."

Bostwick rode to the livery stable, stripped the gear from the roan and rubbed the horse reasonably dry with handfuls of hay, but the ungrateful beast nipped at his elbow and as he departed the stall, took a playful kick at him that he evaded more from habit than attention. Without looking back he slogged through the mud to the saloon. There was no sound from the wagon as he went by.

The Yellowjacket Saloon was a bar fifteen feet long with a row of bottles behind, mud mixed with sawdust on the plank floor and a potbellied stove glowing ruby red like an expectant boil. Behind the bar there was a big man with a polished face and a handlebar mustache. His hair started midway on the top of his head and was jet-black. He had big, square fists and his hands and arms were white as a woman's.

A man dozed in a chair against the wall, his hat over his eyes, another slept with his head on a card table. At the other table four men played a lackluster game in a desultory fashion with a dog-eared deck of cards. From time to time one or the other of them would turn his head to spit at a box of sawdust, and from time to time one of them hit it.

Bostwick removed his hat, slapped the rain drops from it with a blow against his leg and said, "Gimme a shot of rye." The bartender glanced at Jim's broken nose and poured the drink.

A man in a mackinaw who sat near the glowing stove took his pipe from his mouth. "Just the same, I think it's mighty mean of him to take their horses. How are they going to get out of here?"

A man with a streaked blond mustache glanced cynically at the first speaker. "You know Pennock. He doesn't plan for them to leave, not a-tall!"

"He seen that girl," the man in the mackinaw said. "Ain't many women come to Yellowjacket. Besides, that old man was all set to file on Squaw Springs, and Pennock figures that's his'n."

Jim Bostwick downed his drink. Squaw Springs? That was the claim he'd planned to file on.

He let the bartender refill his glass. "He filed on Squaw Springs?"

"Pennock? Why should he? Who's going to butt in when he says it's his'n? They say that gun of his packs seven notches, or could if he wished it."

"It could," the bartender said. "We all know two notches that could go on it. Sandy Chase tried Pennock's game and came up a loser."

"Ought to be a law against killin' when the ground's all froze up. Grave diggin's no pleasure any time, but in frozen ground?"

"Makes for shallow graves," somebody said, "better when Judgment Day comes."

"That girl ain't no more'n sixteen or seventeen. It's a damn shame."

"You go tell that to Pennock."

Nobody replied to that. Well, it was none of his fuss. Besides, they planned to file on his claim, as did Pennock.

"Where's the grub-pile?" he asked.

"Two doors down." He glanced again at the broken nose. "You a fighter?"

Bostwick buttoned his slicker. "Only when I'm pushed."

He started for the door and heard the man in the mackinaw say, "He killed Chase over a woman. What was the other one about?"

"Feller aimed to file on Squaw Springs. Pennock brought some sort of a charge against him, and the feller got riled. Figured he was a tough case and maybe in his home country he was."

"He was too far from home, then. I'm not hunting any beef with Cap Pennock!"

Jim pulled his hat low over his eyes. Shoulders hunched against the rain, he slopped through the mud to the light already showing from the boardinghouse window. The covered wagon was directly across the street and, as he glanced over, he saw the girl getting down from the wagon. Averting his eyes he ducked into the door.

A big-bosomed woman with a red, Irish face pointed at the mat. "Wipe your feet, an' wipe 'em good!"

Meekly, Bostwick did as he was told. Taking off his hat and slicker he hung them from pegs near the door and seated himself at the long table.

"You're early, stranger," the Irish woman said, "but you look hungry, so set up. I'll feed you."

Bostwick looked up as the door closed. It was the girl from the wagon. She had dark hair and large dark eyes. Her face was oval and quite pretty. She had a coffeepot in her hand. She looked at him, then turned hastily away as if she had seen too many of his kind. Bostwick flushed.

"Ma'am? Can I buy some coffee? Grandad's having a chill."

"I shouldn't wonder, sloppin' around in the rain like he's been doin'. You two goin' to pay Cap Pennock what he asks?"

Her lips, delicate as a rose petal, trembled. "We can't. We just don't have it."

The woman filled the coffeepot and waved payment aside. "You take it along, honey. I wouldn't know what to charge for that little dab of coffee."

"But I—! I do want to pay."

"You go along now. It's all right."

When the girl had gone, she brought food to Bostwick. "It's a shame!" she said. "A downright shame!"

Jim Bostwick helped himself to a slab of beef and some mashed potatoes. "Who is this Pennock?" he asked, without looking up.

The woman turned to look at him, seeing only the tangled hair, the blunt, wind-carved unshaved features and the broad, powerful shoulders tapering to narrow hips, shoulders clad in a cheap coat and a wool shirt.

"He's the town marshal. More, he's the boss around here, and folks know it."

"Nobody stands against him?"

"Some tried. Things happened to them. Cap Pennock is a hard man."

He was getting bored by that repeated comment. "When did those folks get here?"

"Yesterday. Pennock took their horses, impounded them for being in the street all night. Back when the mining boom was on, the town council passed that rule because the streets were so crowded at night a body couldn't get through. After the boom died people forgot about it until Pennock was elected marshal, then he dug into the town laws and dug up a lot of regulations, all of which show profit for him."

The door opened and the man in the mackinaw came in followed by his blond-mustached friend. Jim was aware of their attention.

"Howdy, Kate!"

"Howdy, Harbridge! How are you, Grove? How's Emma doin'?"

"Ailin'." Grove replied cheerfully.

The bartender came in and behind him, another man. Talk around the table died and Bostwick looked up. The newcomer was a big man, heavy-shouldered with bold black eyes. Instinctively, Bostwick knew this was Pennock. The man sat down near him and instantly Bostwick felt the stirring of an inner rebellion. There was something deep within him that deeply resented such men.

Bostwick was, as many an American has been before and since, a man who resented authority. He knew its necessity and tried to conform but when that authority became domineering, as this man obviously was, Bostwick's resentment grew.

More than that, very big men who used their size to overawe others, irritated him. That fact accounted for the fact that he had lost as many fights as he had, for he was always choosing the biggest, toughest ones. Large men put him on edge, and he was on edge now.

"Stranger in town?" Pennock asked abruptly.

"No." Bostwick could not have told why he chose to deliberately antagonize the man. "I been in town more'n an hour."

Pennock did not reply, but Bostwick was aware of a subdued stir down the table. He reached over and took the coffeepot almost out of Pennock's hand and filled his cup. The big man's eyes hardened, and he studied Bostwick carefully.

"Don't look at me," Jim said, "I put my horse in the barn."

Somebody snickered and Pennock said, "I didn't ask about your horse. Seems to me, stranger, you're somewhat on the prod."

"Me?" Bostwick looked surprised. "I'm not huntin' trouble. I'm not expectin' trouble, either. Of course, if I was an old man with a pretty young daughter I might feel different."

Pennock put his cup down hard. "I don't like that remark. If you're huntin' trouble you're sure headed right at it."

"I ain't huntin' trouble, but there's no law against a man thinkin' out loud. I'm just of the opinion that a town that will make trouble for a sick old man and his daughter is pretty small stuff."

"Nobody asked you," Pennock said.

Pennock had an ugly expression in his eyes, but Bostwick was suddenly aware that Pennock was in no hurry to push trouble. That was an interesting point. Because he was a stranger? Because the attack had surprised him? Because Pennock was a sure-thing man who had no desire to tackle tough strangers? It was a point worthy of some thought.

Talk started up again, and Kate came around and laid an enormous slab of apple pie on Bostwick's plate. When he looked up, she was smiling.

No man such as Pennock just happens. Each has a past and perhaps somewhere back down the line Pennock was wanted. Or maybe he had taken water for somebody—

"Pennock?" he muttered. "That name does sound familiar." Bostwick looked him over coolly. "Been around here long?"

Pennock's lips thinned out, yet he fought back his anger. "I'll ask the questions here. What do you want in Yellowjacket?"

"Just passin' through."

"A drifter?"

"No, I'm with a big outfit south of here, below the Bradshaws. The Slash Five."

Grove looked up at the mention of the name. "Ain't that the outfit that treed Weaver?"

It had been a fight with some tinhorn gamblers, but Bostwick lied, "We didn't like the town marshal. He gave one of our boys a rough time, so we just naturally moved in."

Kate asked, "What happened to the marshal?"

"Him? Oh, we hung him!" Bostwick said carelessly. "That is, we hung the body. I figure he was already dead because we dropped a loop on him and drug him maybe three hundred yards with some of the boys shootin' into him as we drug him. He was a big feller, too."

"What's that got to do with it?" Pennock's face had lost color but none of the meanness in his eyes.

"Huh? Oh, not much! Only them big fellers don't hang so good. Bodies are too heavy. This feller's head pulled off. Would you believe it? Right off!"

Pete and Shorty would get a boot out of that story. Just wait until he told them! They'd never hung anybody or dragged anybody. A couple of the tinhorns tried to shoot it out but Shorty was, for a cowhand, mighty good with a gun. He nailed one, and Pete wounded the other one. Then they had pitched all the rest of the tinhorns' gear into the street and ran them out of town in their sock feet.

He was aware the others were enjoying his baiting of the town marshal. He was enjoying it himself, and with a good meal inside him he had lost his grouch. But none of this was getting him anywhere closer to Squaw Springs—nor was it getting that girl and her grandad out of trouble.

It was then he remembered they were planning to file on Squaw Springs themselves, so if somehow he got them out of trouble—

He stopped abruptly. Now who said he was getting them out of trouble? What business was it of his? A man could get himself killed, butting into such things.

But saying he did get them out of trouble, then they would be going after the same claim he wanted!

It was a good claim. The spring had a fine flow of excellent water, and the land lay well for farming or grazing. A man could do something with it, fruit trees, maybe. A place like his folks had back East.

Pennock wanted that claim, too, and any way a man looked at it Pennock was in the way.

Cap Pennock finished eating and went outside, ignoring Bostwick. Pennock stopped outside the boardinghouse window picking his teeth with the ivory toothpick that had been hanging from his watchchain. He was looking across the street at the covered wagon. That decided Bostwick. He would get them out of trouble first and then decide about the claim.

"You better lay off Pennock," Harbridge warned him. "He's a killer. He'll be out to get you now, one way or the other."

"He'll get out that book of city laws and find something he can hang onto you."

Bostwick had a sudden thought. "Is there just one of them law books? I mean, does anybody else have a copy?"

"I have, I think," Kate replied dubiously. "My old man was mayor during the boom days. I believe he had one."

"You have a look. I'll talk to that girl."

There was worry in Kate's eyes. "Now you be careful, young man! Don't take Pennock lightly!"

"I surely won't. I ain't anxious to get hurt. You see," he said ruefully, "I had my heart set on Squaw Creek myself!"

He splashed across the street to the wagon and rapped on the wagonbox. Dusk was falling but he could see her expression change from fear to relief as she saw him.

"Ma'am, how much does that marshal want for your horses?"

"He said fifty dollars."

"How's your grandad?"

"Not very good." She spoke softly. "I'm worried."

"Maybe we better get him inside Kate's house. It's cold and damp out here."

"Oh, but we can't! If we leave the wagon the marshal will take it, too."

"You get him fixed to move," Bostwick said. "You leave that marshal to me."

When he explained to Kate she agreed readily but then wondered, "What about the wagon?"

"I'll find a way," he said doubtfully.

"I found that book," Kate said, "for whatever good it will do you."

It was not really a book, just a few handwritten sheets stapled together. It was headed boldly: *City Ordnances*.

Bostwick was a slow reader at best, but he seated himself and began to work his way through the half-dozen pages of what a long-ago town council had decreed for Yellowjacket.

Later, when he had grandad safely installed in the room where Kate's husband had once lived, he had a long talk with Kate.

"I'll do it! I'll do it or me name's not Katie Mulrennan!"


Watching his chance to move unseen, Bostwick ran through the mud and crawled into the wagon, burrowing down amidst the bedding and odds and ends of household furniture. He had been there but a few minutes when he heard a splashing of hoofs and a rattle of trace-chains. Pennock was, as he had expected, hitching grandpa's team to the wagon.

Crouching back of the seat, he waited. Pennock had learned of his moving grandad into Kate's but had no idea Bostwick was inside the wagon.

It was dark and wet, and the big man was watching his footing as he started to clamber into the wagon. He missed seeing the hand that shot out of the darkness and grabbed the lines from his hand, nor the foot until it smashed into his chest.

Pennock let out a choking yell and grabbed at the leg as he toppled backward into the mud.

Scrambling to the seat, Bostwick slapped the horses with the lines, and the heavy wagon started with a jerk.

Behind him there was an angry shout. Glancing back Bostwick saw the big man lunge after the wagon, then slip and fall facedown in the mud. Then the team was running, and the wagon was out of town on the trail to Squaw Springs.

Jim Bostwick drove for thirty minutes until he came to what he was looking for, an abandoned barn that had stood there since boom days. He drove over the gravel approach and into the door in the end of the barn. Fortunately, somebody had used the barn during the summer and there was hay in the mangers. He unhitched the horses and tied them to the manger, and then going outside, he eliminated what tracks he could find. The rain would do the rest.

When he had finished he went back to town riding one horse and leading the other. He took them to the livery stable, then scouted the boardinghouse, but as Kate had foretold, most of the townspeople were present.

When he entered, Cap Pennock half-started to his feet but Bostwick had a thumb hooked in his belt near his gun, and slowly Pennock sat down again.

"You the one who drove that wagon off?"

"I was. And I was completely within my rights."

Astonishment replaced anger on Pennock's face. "What do you mean . . . *rights?*"

"You quiet down, Pennock. We've got business." Bostwick glanced at Kate. "Are you ready, judge?"

"*Judge?*" Pennock's hands rested flat on the table. He looked like an old bull at bay. "What's going on here?"

Kate Mulrennan banged the table with a hammer. "Court's now in session!"

Pennock looked from one to the other. "What kind of tomfoolery is this?" he demanded.

"It means," Bostwick replied, "that the town council met this afternoon and appointed me the town marshal according to the regulation set forth in the city ordnances of Yellowjacket, which decrees—read it, Katie."

> The aforesaid town council shall meet on the fifth day of January, or as soon thereafter as possible, and shall appoint a judge, a town marshal and town clerk. These officials shall hold office only until the fifth of January following, at which time the council shall again meet and reappoint or replace these officials as they shall see fit.

Bostwick's eyes never left Pennock. It was the first time the man's bluff had been called, and he was expecting trouble.

Appointed to the office almost three years before, he had run the town as he saw fit and had pocketed the fines.

"That means," Jim went on, "that you are no longer the town marshal and I am. It also means that for two years you have been acting without authority. As there was no meeting of the town council in that time we will waive that part of it, but we must insist on an accounting of all the fines and monies collected by you."

"What? You're a pack of crazy fools!"

"According to regulations you get ten percent of all collected. Now we want an accounting."

Cap Pennock clutched the edge of the table. Month after month he had bullied these people, fining them as well as strangers, and no man dared deny him. Now this stranger had come to Yellowjacket and in one day his power had crumbled to nothing.

But had it? Need he let it be so? Watching Pennock, Bostwick judged that he had been wary of tackling a tough man who might be a gunfighter, but driven into a corner, Pennock had no choice. It was run or fight.

"I haven't the money." Pennock was very cool now. "So you'll pay hell collecting it."

"We thought of that, so you have a choice. Pay up or leave town tomorrow by noon."

"Suppose I decide to pay no attention to this kangaroo court?"

"Then it becomes my job," Bostwick replied quietly, "as the newly elected town marshal . . ."

Cap Pennock got to his feet. Bostwick had to hand it to him. When the chips were down Pennock was going to fight for what he had. "You won't have to come looking for me, Bostwick. I'll be out there waiting for you."

Pennock started for the door and Kate called out, "Hold up a minute, Cap! You owe me a dollar for grub. Now pay up, you cheapskate!"

Pennock's face was livid. He hesitated, then livid with anger he tossed a dollar on the table and walked out.

"Well, Jim," Harbridge said, "you said if it came to this that you'd handle it. Now you've got it to do.

"He's a dangerous man with a gun. Sandy Chase was good, but he wasn't good enough. I never would've had the nerve to go through with this if Kate hadn't told us you'd face him, if need be."

"Are you fast?" Grove asked.

"No, I'm not. Probably I'm no faster than any of you, but I'll be out there and he'd better get me quick or I'll take him."

Bostwick disliked to brag, but these men needed to believe. If he failed them they would take the brunt of Pennock's anger.

When they had trooped out of the room and gone to their homes, Bostwick sat down again, suddenly scared. He looked up to see Ruth watching him.

"I heard what you said. You've done this for me . . . for us, haven't you?"

Bostwick's hard features flushed. "Ma'am, I ain't much, and I'm no braver than most, it's just that when I see a man like him something gets into me."

"I wish we had a few more like you!" Kate said.

She gestured to the table. "You set, I've some more of that pie." She looked around at Ruthie. "You, too, you look like you could do with some nourishment."

When the sun hung over the street, Bostwick stood in a doorway thinking what a damned fool he was. Why, Shorty, who laid no claims to being good with a gun, was better than he was. Yet he had walked into this with his eyes open.

He must make no effort at a fast draw. He was not fast, and he would be a fool to try. He must accept the fact that he was going to be hit, and he must hope that the first shot didn't kill him.

He might have time for one shot only, and he must be sure that shot would kill. Jim Bostwick was a man without illusions. He knew he was going to take some lead, and he had to be prepared for it. Yet he was a tough man, hard years of work and brutal fights had proved that. He was going to have to take some lead and keep a'coming.

He was a good shot with a pistol, better than most when shooting at targets, only this time the target would be shooting back.

The sun was baking the wetness from the street and from the false-fronted buildings. Somewhere a piano was playing. He stepped into the street.

*"Bostwick!"*

The call was from *behind* him! Cap Pennock had been lurking somewhere near the livery stable and had outsmarted him, played him for a sucker.

Cap was standing there, big and rough, a pistol in his hand. And he was smiling at the success of his trick. Cap fired.

*Take your time!* The words rang in his mind like a bell. He lifted his bone-handled gun and fired just as Cap let go with his second shot. Something slugged Bostwick in the leg as he realized Cap had missed his first shot!

His eyes were on that toothpick on Cap's watch-chain. He squeezed off a shot even as he fell, then he was getting up, bracing himself for a careful shot.

Cap seemed to be weaving, turning his side to him like a man on a dueling field. Bostwick fired from where his gun was, shooting as a man points a finger. This time there was no mistake. Where the toothpick had hung there was a widening stain now, and he fired again, then went to his knees, losing his grip on his gun.

Somewhere a door slammed, and he heard running feet. He reached out for his gun, but his hand closed on nothing. He smelled the warm, wet earth on which his face rested, and he felt somebody touch his shoulder.

"I think he's waking up," somebody said, some woman.

He moved then and a bed creaked and when his eyes opened he was looking up at a ceiling and he heard Ruthie saying, "Oh, Katie! He's awake! He's awake!"

"Awake and hungry," he grumbled.

He looked at Ruthie. "How's your grandad?"

"He died . . . only a little while after your fight. He said you were a good man."

"Cap Pennock? Did I—?"

"You hit him four times. He's been buried these two weeks."

"*Two weeks?* You mean I've been here two weeks?"

"You have. Two weeks and a day, to be exact." She took his hand. "Jim? Kate told me that you planned to file on Squaw Springs yourself."

"Forget it. That will be a good place for you and as for me, I'm just a forty-dollar-a-month cowhand."

"We could do it together."

"Well, you know how folks talk. You being a young girl, and all."

"What if we were married?" she suggested doubtfully.

"Well," he admitted cautiously, "that might do it." He stole a look at her from the corners of his eyes. "Did you ever take a good look at me? Even when I'm shaved—"

"You are shaved, silly!" She laughed at him. "Kate shaved you. She said she always wondered what you looked like under all that brush."

He lifted a hand. It was true. He had been shaved. "You think you could marry a man like me?"

"Well," she said, "just to stop the talk—"

# MERRANO OF THE DRY COUNTRY

Nobody even turned a head to look his way as Barry Merrano entered the store. They knew he was there, and their hatred was almost tangible, he felt it pushing against him as he walked to the counter.

Mayer, who kept the store, was talking to Tom Drake, owner of the TD and considered the wealthiest man in the valley; Jim Hill, acknowledged to be its first settler; and Joe Stangle, from the head of the valley. After a moment Mayer left them and walked over to him.

The storekeeper's lips offered no welcoming smile although Barry thought he detected a faint gleam of sympathy in the man's eyes.

In a low voice, Barry gave his order, and several times the others glanced his way, for they could still overhear a part of what he was saying and he was ordering things they could no longer afford.

"I'll have to ask for cash," Mayer said. "With the drouth and all, money's short."

37

Barry felt a sudden surge of anger. There was a moment when he thought to bring their world crashing about them by asking how long it had been since the others had paid cash. He knew what it would mean. Suddenly they would be faced with the harsh reality of their situation. The Mirror Valley country was broke . . . flat broke.

No sooner had the feeling come than it passed. He had no desire for revenge. They hated him, and he knew why they hated him. They hated him because he was the son of Miguel Merrano, the Mexican vaquero who married the most beautiful and sought-after girl in the valley. They hated him because he had the audacity to return after they had driven his father from the area. They hated him because when they built a fence to keep his cattle from water he had found water elsewhere. Worst of all, he himself had kept up the fence they built, building it even stronger.

They hated him because he had the nerve to tell them they were ruining their land, and that drouth would come and their cattle would die.

"That's all right," he told Mayer, "I have the money and I can pay."

He took his order and paid for it with three gold pieces placed carefully on the counter. Joe Stangle looked at the gold, then stared at him, his eyes mean. "I'd like to know," he said, "where a greaser gets that kind of money. Maybe the sheriff should do some looking around!"

Barry gathered his armful of groceries and put them in a burlap sack. "Maybe he could"—he spoke gently—"and maybe you could, too, Joe. All you'd have to do would be to use your eyes."

He went out, then returned for a second and a third load. "That greaser father of yours knowed what he was doin' when he bought that land," Stangle said.

"The land my father bought was the same sort of land you all have. Once there was good grass everywhere but you overstocked your land and fed it out of existence. Then the brush came in and the underlying roots killed off more grass. When the grass thinned out your stock started eating poison weeds.

There's nothing wrong with your land that a few good years won't cure."

"We heard all that preachin' before. No greaser's goin' to come around and tell me how to run my range! Jim Hill an' me were runnin' cattle before you was born!"

Merrano took his last armful of groceries and turned toward the door. White with fury, Joe Stangle stuck out his foot and Barry tripped and sprawled on the floor, spilling his groceries.

Nobody laughed. Tom Drake threw an irritated glance at Stangle, but said nothing.

Barry Merrano got up. His face was very cold and still. "That was a cheap thing to do, Stangle," he said. "There's not much man in you, is there?"

Had he been slapped across the mouth it would have been easier to take. Stangle trembled, and his hand dropped to his gun. Only Jim Hill's grabbing his arm prevented him from shooting Merrano in the back as he walked out the door.

"Yellow!" Stangle sneered. "Yellow, like any greaser!"

"You're wrong, Joe," Hill said quietly, "he's not yellow, nor was his old man."

"He run, didn't he?" Stangle said. "He quit, didn't he?" His voice was hoarse with hatred.

"Yes, he left, but if I recall correctly he backed you down, Joe."

Stangle's face was livid, but Hill turned his back on him and asked Mayer, "I'll have to ask for credit again, Mayer. Can you carry me?"

"I always have." Mayer tried to smile. He had carried them all, but how much longer he could afford to do it he did not know. Only the cash Barry Merrano had spent with him enabled him to meet his own bills, but scarcely that.

Barry Merrano's buckboard rattled out of town, hitting the long, dry road to Willow Springs. It was almost sundown but heat lay over Mirror Valley like a sodden thing, dust hanging heavy in the air. It was always here now, that dust. A few years back, his mother told him, this valley had been a green and lovely place. There had been fat cattle around then, and it was here she had met his father, that pleasant-faced, friendly

Mexican—slim, wiry, and elegant—and it was here they had courted and here they were married.

"I'm glad she didn't live to see it," Barry muttered, "it would have broken her heart."

In the rush to get rich from beef cattle the grass had been overgrazed, and the creosote, cat-claw, and tarweed had started to move in. The grass had grown thinner. It had been eaten down, and worn down, wind had whipped the dust from around the roots and rains had washed out the clumps of grass. The water holes, once plentiful, never seemed to fill up or remain full anymore.

"Climate's changing," Drake had suggested to Hill, and the latter nodded his agreement.

"Don't ever recall it being so dry," Hill added.

They watched with sullen impatience when Barry Merrano returned to occupy his father's ranch. And they turned away in contempt when he told them the climate was not changing, but they were simply running more cattle than the range would support.

Willow Springs loomed before him, and Barry kept his eyes averted. It was at Willow Springs where his father and mother first met. It had been green and lovely then, and the pool had been wide and deep. Now most of the willows were dead and where the pool had been, the earth was cracked and gray. There had been no water since early summer.

Turning right at Willow Springs his road became a climb. It was only a trail, two winding ruts across the parched plain. Ahead of him he saw The Fence.

All over the country it was known by no other name. It was simply The Fence, only nowadays it was mentioned rarely.

Seven ranchers had built The Fence, and they had built it when Barry refused to leave.

That was four years ago but to Barry it seemed longer. He had returned, knowing every detail of the hatred Mirror Valley people had felt for his father. He was determined to face it down and win a place for himself; and the land his father left him was all he had. He turned up the draw toward the house

Miguel Merrano had built in the basin under the shoulder of Table Mountain.

Three days after his arrival a dozen horsemen had ridden up the draw to tell him he was not wanted. They wanted no Mexicans in Mirror Valley.

He had waited in the door, listening. And then he smiled, looking much more like his Irish mother at that moment. "I'm sorry you've had your ride for nothing," he said. "I'm staying."

"Get out or we'll run you out!" Stangle had shouted.

"Then why waste time talking?" Merrano suggested. "Why don't you start your running?"

With an oath, Stangle had reached for his gun, but his hand got no farther than the butt, then very, very carefully he moved his hand away. Not one of them saw where Merrano had held the shotgun, but suddenly it was there, in Merrano's hands.

"Sorry, gentlemen, but I don't like being shot at. I am not a man of violence, but I've several thousand rounds of ammunition and I hit what I shoot at.

"I've noticed that a shotgun has a depressing effect on violent men, as nobody can tell just who is going to get himself ripped open. Now, gentlemen, I've a lot of work to do. Do you go cheerfully or do I have to start a graveyard?"

They went, and Joe Stangle was not the last to leave.

Three days later they built The Fence. They built it across the draw that led from Merrano's adobe in the basin to town. They built it horse-high, hog-tight, and bull-strong. Then six men waited with rifles for somebody to try cutting The Fence.

Barry Merrano came down the draw in his buckboard, and they picked up their rifles for a killing. Before he came to The Fence, Barry pulled up and tumbled a roll of barbed wire from the back of the buckboard. Then, as they watched, suddenly feeling very foolish, Barry Merrano built his own fence, higher, stronger, and tighter. In place of their nine strands of wire he put up fourteen. In the forty feet of width across the draw he put up nine posts to their five. Then he got into his buckboard and drove away.

Cab Casady, forty-five, and accounted one of the toughest

men in the valley, laughed. Just as suddenly as he began laughing, he stopped. "We're a pack of fools!" he said with disgust. "And for one, I'm ashamed of myself! I'm going home!"

Avoiding each other's eyes the others went to their horses, mounted up and rode away. The Fence was a topic no longer mentioned in conversation.

Yet all wondered what Merrano would do, for there was no way out of the basin unless one walked. For three weeks they waited, and then one day Barry Merrano drove into town for supplies. When they rode out to see, The Fence was still intact.

Jim Hill, although he would not admit it, was relieved. Yet like the others, he was curious. He mounted up and scouted around the country. It was almost a month after that he rode into town. He had a drink in the Faro House and said, "Do you know what that Mex did? He's bored him a hole through the Neck!"

Anybody but Jim Hill they would have called a liar. The Neck was a wall of rock that joined the bulk of Table Mountain to the rest of the range, yet when they rode out to see it, there was a black hole in that red wall of rock.

How could it have been done? It was impossible, yet it had been done.

Nobody mentioned fencing the tunnel mouth.

A few days later when he passed Willow Springs, Barry Merrano saw a rider emerge from the shabby little grove and start across the trail. When she saw him, she pulled up.

It was Candy Drake.

He stopped the buckskins when he drew close. "How are you, ma'am?" He touched his hat. He started to comment on the heat and the drouth but thought the better of it. Instead he indicated the pinto's leg. "I see that leg is coming along all right."

"Yes, it got well just like you said it would."

He wanted to talk, yet wanted to avoid anything that might give offense. Candy Drake was the prettiest girl in Mirror Valley. He had talked to no one in almost three months, and he admitted to himself that he had been in love with Candy Drake for three years.

"The drouth came the way you said it would, too," she said almost accusingly. "Everything seems to turn out the way you say it will."

He flushed slightly. "Anybody who took the time to look could see this country was in trouble," he said. "This country had been so overgrazed there was no grass to hold what moisture we got. Most of it could have been prevented if work had been started a couple of years ago."

He took off his hat and ran his fingers through his thick, dark hair. "Nobody would listen to me when I offered to help. I was just that damned greaser son of Molly O'Brien's, so what could I know?"

There was a bitterness in his voice that came through no matter how hard he tried to hold it back. He had lived too close to this for too long a time.

Mirror Valley had been outraged when pretty Molly O'Brien had married Miguel Merrano. He had been a top-hand, hired only for the roundup. Pete Drake had his eyes on Molly, and so had others, but she had made promises to no one until she met Merrano.

Miguel bought the Table Mountain place and for four bitter years struggled against the hatred and the prejudice directed against them. Finally, when young Barry was almost two, they had gone away.

Surprisingly, they prospered. Barry heard many tales of Mirror Valley as he was growing up but nothing of the reason for leaving until he was fifteen. He determined then to return and fight it out if it took twenty years.

"My father certainly should know how to run cattle," Candy protested. "He's raised more cattle than you have ever seen."

"I'm twenty-six," Barry said, "and I've a lot to learn, but simply growing old doesn't make one wise. Your father came into a rich, new country and nothing could convince him it would not always stay rich.

"The others were the same. They ran more cattle than the

range could support. Once when I was visiting at your place I tried to suggest some changes, but he just thought me a fool."

"But Barry," she protested, "millions of buffalo used to run on these plains, so how could they be spoiled by a few thousand cattle?"

"Your father said the same thing," Barry said, "but you both forget that the buffalo never stopped moving as they grazed. They were constantly moving and as they moved on, the grass had a chance to grow back before they returned again. Now the range is fenced and the cattle are continually feeding over the same ground."

Candy was exasperated. "We always have the same argument," she protested. "Can you talk of anything else?"

"Many things, if you'll listen. Candy, why don't you come over to my place and see for yourself?"

"To your place?" She was shocked, yet as the idea took hold, she was intrigued. Like all in the valley she was curious. What was he doing back there? Nobody had visited the basin since he took over, and they all knew Barry Merrano paid cash for everything. How could he do it?

That he ran cattle, they all knew. He had driven cattle into Aragon to sell and Aragon was out of the way for people from the valley. They knew he did it to avoid meeting them.

"It wouldn't be proper," she said, but as she said it she knew it was a feeble excuse. She had done many things that were often considered improper. "Anyway, that dark tunnel would frighten me. However did you make it?"

"It was not hard. Want to come?"

Her father's disapproval and what might be considered proper was opposed to her curiosity, which resulted in a sweeping victory . . . for her curiosity.

Interested in spite of herself, she followed along. He drove the buckskins into the dark tunnel, and she fell in behind them. The buckskins trotted along undisturbed by the darkness until rounding a small curve they saw light before them. When she emerged from the tunnel she pulled up with a gasp.

The first impression was of size. She had thought of the basin as a small place, yet there must have been thousands of acres within that circle of hills. When she looked again she saw nothing was as it had been.

The basin, in contrast to the country she had left, was green and lovely. A winding road led to a stone cottage that stood on a wide ledge and on either side of the road there were fenced fields, the one on the right of clover, on the left of corn, and the corn was shoulder high as she rode past it on her horse.

The old trees she remembered from a time she had come here as a child, when it was abandoned, but there were younger trees, including a small orchard, carefully set out. The valley of the basin itself was green, with here and there a small pool that caught the sunlight.

"Is that *grass* down there?"

"Most of it. Some is black grama, some is curly mesquite grass. It has always grown in this country but I am careful not to overgraze it. The basin opens at the other end into a canyon and then into Long Valley, the old Navajo sheep range. I made a deal with the Navajo to graze some of it. I run about fifteen head to the section but actually most of this will support twice as many."

Her father should see this, she thought. He would never believe it if she told him.

"But what about water? Where do you get water?"

"This country never has enough, and most of the rain comes in late summer. When I came back I already knew the problem I faced. I did some blasting, built three dams the first summer, damming three draws that open into the basin. Wherever I found a low spot I made some kind of a reservoir. Now I have a couple of small lakes behind the dams and there are pools scattered all over the basin and down into Long Valley. Toward the end of summer most of them do dry up, but by that time the rains are not far off.

"In this country water runs off the hills like off a tin roof so you have to save what you can. Of course, I've drilled a couple of wells, too."

Amazed, she listened with only half her attention. Suddenly, she was frightened. If Joe Stangle saw this place his hatred and envy would be doubled.

She thought of something she had wondered about. "Barry? However did you make that tunnel?"

He chuckled. "Candy, over two-thirds of it was a big, natural cave. I paced it off, then went on top and measured the rock and found I only had a little way to go and much was an upthrust from below that I could take off with a pick.

"As far as the grass goes, I never graze much stock on it at any one time, and I shift them around to give the grass a chance to grow back."

"Don't you have trouble with old Two Moons?"

"Not at all. I explained what I had in mind, and he understood right away. The Navajo have always understood grazing pretty well, and I offered them a fair price."

As they walked back her eyes strayed toward the house. She would have liked to see the inside, but he did not suggest it.

He stripped the harness from the team and turned them into the corral, then saddled a horse. "It's getting late," he said, "I'll ride home with you."

The ride to the TD was silent, for neither felt like talking. Barry was happy and miserable at the same time. He was in love with Candy, but her father had been one of those who tried to drive him off the place, and her father had lent his tacit consent to building The Fence, if no more than that.

The feeling against him had grown stronger rather than otherwise. The incident in the store would make them turn even further away, and as none of them liked him, most would be only too quick to accept his walking away from Stangle as cowardice.

When they drew up at the gate he said, "I wish you'd come again. And bring your father."

"He wouldn't come, Barry." She was puzzled about her feelings toward him. He had talked more than ever before, and for the first time she had seen something of the kind of man he was, yet she could not quite understand him. He was, she suspected, a much more complex human being than any she had known.

"You're beautiful, Candy." The words came so suddenly that

she looked up, surprised by them. "You're so beautiful it hurts. I wish—"

A dark figure loomed near the gate. "Candy? Is that you? Who's that with you?"

"Price? I was just saying good night to Barry Merrano."

"*Who?*" Astonishment mingled with anger. "Has that dirty Mex been botherin' you? If he has, I'll—!"

"I simply rode home with Miss Drake," Barry said. "There's no reason to get excited."

Price Taylor shoved open the gate and came out. "Listen, greaser! You turn that horse and cut loose for home! Don't you be tellin' me not to get excited! I'll take you off that horse and beat your skull in!"

"Price!" Candy exclaimed. "This is outrageous!"

Taylor was beside Barry's horse. He was a large, somewhat top-heavy young man. As foreman of the TD he had become almost one of the family and he had long looked upon Candy Drake as someone very special and reserved for him, although he had had no encouragement from her and certainly none from Tom Drake, who would have been appalled at the thought. Seeing her in the moonlight with Merrano turned him ugly.

"This is no business for womenfolk! You get along to the house now. I'll take care of this!"

He reached a big hand for Barry and Barry went, much faster than Taylor expected. As Taylor laid hold of him Barry swung his other leg over the saddle and drove his heel into the bigger man's chest, sending him staggering. Then he dropped to the ground.

Coolly, he waited until Taylor recovered his balance. "I'd rather you'd go along to the house," Barry said, "but if you want a licking you can have it."

"A lickin'? *Me?*" Taylor's size had won several brawls for him, and he fancied himself a tough man.

He started for Merrano and a stiff left stopped him, smashing his lips. Taylor dropped into a half-crouch, arms wide to grapple, and moved in. Barry caught the larger man's sleeve and jerked him forward, off-balance, then kicked his foot from under him. Taylor sprawled forward, falling on his hands and knees.

Merrano stood waiting, and Taylor came half erect, then launched himself in a long dive. Merrano sidestepped and waited.

Slowly, carefully, Taylor got up from the ground. Putting his fists in front of him in an awkward simulation of a boxer, he moved in. Merrano moved to the side and Taylor caught him on the cheekbone with a clumsy swing, but Merrano stood his ground and struck three hard, fast blows to the body, then an uppercut thrown in close that tipped Taylor's chin back.

Taylor bored in, swinging wildly. Another punch caught Barry but again he failed to step back and, moving in, sank a wicked right into Taylor's belly and hooked a left to his face.

Taylor turned, Barry feinted a left and Taylor pawed at the air to knock the punch down, but the feint was followed by a stiff left, then another and another. Taylor was big, but lacked any semblance of fighting skill. He came in, legs spread wide, swinging. Barry hit him with a left, then knocked him down with a right. Taylor got up slowly and Barry knocked him down again.

Taylor got to his knees but was unable to get to his feet. "I'm sorry, Taylor, but you asked for it. You're a game man, but you're no fighter."

Taylor made it to his feet, weaving. Barry thrust out a hand. "As far as I'm concerned, there's no hard feelings. Will you shake?"

Price Taylor ignored the out-thrust hand.

Barry swung to the saddle. "I'm sorry, Candy. I didn't want this to happen."

"You'd better go," she replied coldly.

He swung his horse and rode away, cutting across the plains, gray and empty under a wide white moon.

Taylor wiped his face. "You must think I'm an awful bust, gettin' whipped that way."

Candy shook her head soberly. "No, Price, I don't, but I think we've all made an awful mistake!"

Taylor grunted. "Looks like I made one, anyway."

\*        \*        \*

When she opened the door into the wide living room of the ranch house Candy was surprised to find five or six men talking with her father. Jim Hill was there, and Joe Stangle. Also there were Cab Casady, Rock Dulin, Vinnie Lake, Hardy Benson and a big, powerful man whom she did not know.

"We've got to figure out something or we're finished," Benson was saying. "My cattle are dying like flies!"

"Mine, too," Stangle said, "water holes are dry, and there's no grass."

"If you ask me," Dulin commented, "it ain't only the drouth. There's been some rustlin'."

"There's been no rustling in this country since we got rid of Bert Scovey and his outfit."

"That greaser always has money," Stangle said. "Where's he get it?"

"If you could see that Basin Ranch of his," Candy interrupted, "you wouldn't wonder. You should all have listened to him a long time ago."

Her father looked up sharply. "Candy? What makes you say that? When did you see it?"

"Today," she replied calmly. "He invited me to see it and I did."

"You went into the basin with that low-down Mex?"

"Hold on a minute, Tom!" Stangle lifted a hand. "You mean he's got grass?"

"Yes, he has!" Candy was pleased with the effect of her words. "The whole basin is green and beautiful! He's got water, and lots of it. He's dammed some of the draws, he's dug out some pools, and he has a lot of water. He's even got a grain crop!"

"Grain?" Hill exclaimed. "You mean he's farmin'?"

"Not farming, just raising enough for his own stock. He told me he fed during the winter or just before taking them to market."

"You actually *saw* water and grass?" Hill asked.

"He's done nothing you all couldn't have done, and he's done it all in four years! Certainly, I saw it!"

"You takin' up for him now?" Dulin asked.

"No! I am just telling you he's proved his case. He was right, and you all were wrong."

Stangle leaned forward, intent. "Where'd you say that water was? In Cottonwood Draw?"

"He's dammed both Cottonwood and Spring Valley. He's planted seedling trees around them to hold the banks and help conserve moisture."

"Well!" Stangle slapped his thigh. "That's it, men! That settles our problem!"

"What do you mean?" Drake looked up hopefully.

"He's got water. Why don't we just take down The Fence and drive our cattle in there? That sneakin' Mexican's got no right to all that water when our cattle are dyin'!"

Casady let his chair legs down hard. "You mean to say you'd have the gall to ask him for water after the way we've treated him?"

"Ask nothin'!" Stangle said. "Just tear down The Fence and let our cattle in. They'd find the water and grass soon enough."

"We couldn't do that," Drake protested, "it wouldn't be right."

"Right?" Stangle's voice was hoarse with bitterness. "Are you so anxious to go broke? You want to watch your cattle die?"

"You'd do a thing like that?" Casady demanded, his eyes going from one to the other.

"I would," Rock Dulin said. "Are you too nice to save your cows?"

Candy stared at Dulin, appalled.

"No, Rock," Casady said quietly, "I'm not too nice. I hope, however, that I know something of fair play. We've bucked that kid and made his life pure hell. We tried to drive him out and he stuck. We fenced him out of our country and still he stayed. He tried to tell us, and we were too damned hard-headed to listen. Now, you would ruin what he has done. How long will that little grass last if we turn our herds in there? We've got seven or eight thousand head between us."

"I don't know, and I don't give a damn!" Stangle said. "He's got no place here in the first place. I've got my cattle to save, and I'll save them."

"He won't stand for it," Hill replied. "He'll fight."

"I hope he does!" Stangle said. "Him and his highfalutin ways! Handin' gold right over the counter! Throwin' it right in our faces!"

"What if he does fight?" Drake asked.

"You fought injuns to get there, didn't you?" Dulin said. "You killed some of Scovey's boys?"

Candy Drake stared in shocked disbelief. "You could do a thing like *that*? Joe Stangle, what kind of a man are you? To wreck all he's done! To destroy everything!"

"It would save our stock, Miss Candy," Benson protested. "We've families to think about. Your pa's in the same fix I am, and I'm head over heels in debt."

"What would you do if he wasn't there? What if I'd not been so foolish as to tell you?"

"But he is there," Dulin replied, "and thanks to you, we know what he's got. There may be water enough to keep our stock alive for a month, and by then the rains might come. I'm for it."

"So am I!" Stangle declared.

"It isn't right," Drake protested. "If he has water it's due to his own hard work, and the water's his."

"Well, Tom, if you want to go broke, the choice is yours," Stangle said. "I'll be damned if I let my cattle die. If you had a water hole you'd let me use it, wouldn't you? Why should he be the only one who's fenced in?"

Casady's dislike was obvious as he stared at Stangle. "And just who built The Fence? Seems to me you had a hand in it, Stangle."

"That cuts no ice." Stangle waved a hand. "We'll tear it down. We'll run our cattle in there, and then we'll see what happens. I'm not going to let my cattle die because he keeps his water fenced up."

"I reckon that speaks for me." Hardy Benson spoke reluctantly. "I'm in debt. I'll lose all I have."

"That says it for me," Vinnie Lake added.

Cab got to his feet. "How about you, Tom?"

Drake hesitated, before his eyes the vision of his dying cattle, the size of the bill he owed Mayer.

"I'll string with the boys," he said.

For a moment Casady looked around at their faces. "I'd rather my cattle died," he said. "Good night, *gentlemen!*"

Dulin started to his feet, his hand reaching for his gun. "I'll kill that—"

"Better not try," Hill said dryly. "You never saw the day you could match Cab with a gun."

He looked around at their faces. "I don't know that I like this, myself."

"It's settled," Stangle declared. "Dulin, Lake, Benson, Drake, and Hill. How about you, McKesson?"

"Sure, I'll ride along, trail my stock with yours. I never liked that Mex, no way."

Tom Drake glanced at him thoughtfully. Curt McKesson was a new man in the valley, a big, somber man with a brooding, sullen face. Drake had seen him angry but once, but that had revealed him to have a vicious, murderous temper. He had beaten a horse to death before anyone could interfere. He disliked the man, and it disturbed him to see how McKesson's eyes followed Candy every move she made. The light in them was not good to see.

Joe Stangle got up, satisfaction showing in his eyes and voice. "We can meet at Willow Springs Monday morning. Once The Fence is down and the cattle started for water there will be no stoppin' them."

Candy watched, feeling sick and empty. She wanted to protest but knew they would not listen. Their own desperation coupled with Stangle's hatred and Dulin's sullen brutality had led them into something most of them would live to regret. Now they were only thinking about delaying their bad times. One by one they filed out and when they had gone she turned on her father.

"Dad, you've got to stop them! You can't let them destroy all that poor boy's work!"

"Poor boy, is it? He's got no right to all that water when our cattle are dying!"

"Who dammed those draws? What have you done to try to

save your cattle? All you've done is sit here with the rest of them and sneer at what he thought and what he did!"

"Be quiet!" Drake's voice boomed, his guilt making him even more angry. "I won't have you takin' up for that Mexican. Nor is it your place to question my actions."

"Dad"—Candy's tone was cold—"you'd better understand this. Barry Merrano will fight. If he fights, somebody will get killed. If I were you I'd do a lot of thinking before you start anything. It isn't like it was when you drove out those rustlers. The country has changed."

Despite himself, he knew what she said was the truth. He shook his head irritably. "Nonsense! He's yellow! He won't fight."

He hesitated, thinking. Then he said, "He won't fight. Joe Stangle made a fool of him and he did nothing, nothing at all!"

"Then you'd better go out to the bunkhouse and take a look at Price Taylor. Price thought he wouldn't fight, too."

"What? What do you mean?"

"Barry rode home with me tonight and was leaving me at the gate. He had been a gentleman, no more. Price jumped him, and Barry gave him a beating."

"He whupped Price? Girl, you're crazy!"

"Go look at him. Ask Price if he's yellow. Also, I seem to remember you tried to frighten him away before, and he didn't run. He had only an idea to fight for then. Now he's got a place worth having!"

She paused. "Remember this, Dad. He'll fight, and somebody will get killed."

"Bah!" Drake said, but he was disturbed. She knew her father well enough to know that he had not liked the action taken tonight, yet these were the men he knew, men he had worked beside, men with whom he had shared trouble. He had gone along because it offered a way out of bankruptcy and failure, and because there seemed no alternative.

Tom Drake had fought Indians, outlaws, and rustlers, and now he would fight to hold the place, but he knew in his heart that if he were Merrano, he would fight. He did not approve of killing and he believed Merrano would run, yet now, listening to his daughter, he was no longer so sure.

"Dad?" Candy spoke quietly. "I want you to understand. If you go through with this I'll go and fight beside Barry Merrano. I will take a rifle and stand beside him and what happens to him will happen to me."

"*What!*" He stared at his daughter, consternation in his eyes. In that instant he looked not only into his daughter's eyes but into those of his wife, and something more, he saw a reflection of himself, thirty years before.

Without another word, Candy turned and left the room. The big old man behind her stared after her, hurt, confusion, and doubt struggling in his mind. He sat down suddenly in the big hide chair.

Suddenly he felt old and tired, staring into the fire, trying to think things out and seeing only his dying cattle and the failure of all he had done. The cracked mud in the dried-up water holes, the leafless trees, all his years, all his struggle, all his work and his plans gone.

That was Friday night. Early Saturday morning a buckboard left Mirror Valley and bounced over the stones and through the thick gray dust toward Willow Springs and the turnoff to Merrano's tunnel. Clyde Mayer had made a decision, and he was following through. He knew nothing of the action taken by the ranchers at the TD ranch. He was threatened by foreclosure by the wholesalers, and in this emergency he was turning to the one man in the valley who seemed to have money.

The tunnel was unguarded, and he turned in hesitantly. When he emerged into the bright sunlight Barry Merrano was standing in the door of his house. The sound of hoofs in the tunnel was plainly audible within the house at any time.

Mayer pulled up in the ranch yard and tied the lines to the whipstock. He got down carefully, for he was not as agile as he had once been.

"Howdy, son!" He peered at Barry over his glasses. "Reckon this visit's a surprise."

"Come in," Barry invited. "I'm just back from patching a

hole in a dam. A badger dug into it, and the water started to drain out."

"My, my!" Mayer looked around slowly. "Your mother would be right proud, young man! Right proud! She was a fine woman, your mother was!"

"Thanks. That's always good to hear from somebody else. She was a good mother to me."

When they were seated over coffee, Mayer said, "Son, I've come to you for help. The wholesalers have shut off my credit, and they are demanding money. I am low on stock, and the ranchers will be coming in for supplies."

"How much do you need?"

"An awful lot, son. I'd need five thousand dollars. I'd sell you a half interest in my business for it. I know I've been foolish to extend credit, but these are good men, son, and basically they mean well. Every one of them will pay off if it is the last thing they do, but that won't help me now . . . nor them."

"If you don't get the money, you go broke?"

"That's right."

"Then what happens to the ranchers?"

"They'd starve or get out. The drouth's hit this country so bad there isn't a head of cattle fit to sell. It will take two really good years to get them out of the hole they're in. They'd never be able to stick it out. They have no food, no feed, no water."

Merrano stared into his cup, his brown, wind-tanned face thoughtful. After a moment he said, "All right. I'll buy a half interest in your store on one condition. I don't want anybody to know about it."

Mayer hesitated. "What about credit for the ranchers? They are my friends, and I'd hate to turn them down."

"Don't. Give them what they need. Somebody has to have faith in this country. Maybe after this they will learn their lesson and handle their stock sensibly."

Mayer stood up, his relief obvious. "I don't mind telling you, son, I was scared. I hadn't anywhere to turn."

He started for his buckboard and paused before getting into

it. "Son, you be careful. That Joe Stangle is a mighty mean man, and so is Dulin."

"Thanks. I'll keep my eyes open."

After Mayer had gone Barry returned to the house and got his Winchester. Then he slipped on his gunbelt. It was time to begin moving the cattle off the Long Valley range and back into the basin. No use to let them feed there too long. In a few weeks he would take thirty head over to Aragon for sale. It would save on feed and water and give him a little more working cash.

He had saddled up and was about to mount when he heard a rattle of horse's hoofs. It was Candy Drake.

At her expression he caught her hand. "Candy? What's happened?"

Swiftly, the words tumbling into one another, she told him of the meeting and its result. "Please, Barry! Don't think too hard of Father! All he can see now is his cattle dying!"

"I know," he agreed. "The trouble is that the little water I have wouldn't help much. With that mass of cattle coming in, my smaller pools would be trampled into mud within hours and the bigger pools behind the dams would last no time at all. It would simply add my ruin to the rest of them. Believe me, Candy, I'd like to help.

"There is a way, if they will work. There's water in the White Horse Hills. It would take a lot of work, but they could get at it."

"They wouldn't listen, Barry. Not now."

"There's only one thing I can do now, Candy. They broke my mother's heart on this ground, and they turned Father from a laughter-loving young vaquero into a morose and lonely man.

"There's only one thing I can do, and that's what your father would do or any of the men with him. I am going to fight."

He waved a hand. "There's four years of blood, sweat, and blisters in this. Days and nights when I was so bitterly lonely I thought I'd go insane. I built those dams with my own hands. I gathered the stones for this house, cut and shaped the planks for the floors. I made the chairs. These things are mine, and I'll fight to keep them.

"If a single cow crosses The Fence, that cow will cross over my dead body, but believe me, it won't be lying there alone. Candy, if you can talk to your father, tell him that. Blood won't save his cattle, but if it is blood he wants, that's what he will get."

"They'll kill you, Barry. There are too many of them."

"I won't be alone. This may sound silly, but my mother and father will be with me. This land was theirs before it was mine. The ghosts of a thousand other men who fought for their homes will be there, too!"

"Barry, I told Father that if he came I'd fight with you."

Surprised, he looked up at her. "You said *that*?"

"I did, and I meant it."

Speechless, he hesitated, then shook his head. "No, as much as I'd like it, I can't let you fight against your father. This is my fight. I am obliged for the warning, but you'd better ride on now. But no matter what happens, I'll not forget this."

"All right, I'll go, but Barry, be careful! Joe Stangle hates you! And that other man, Curt McKesson . . . he frightens me!"

For a long time after she was gone, Barry sat staring down the valley, thinking. He would leave the cattle where they were.

Accustomed to working and planning alone he now turned all his thoughts to defense. It was a problem he had considered since his first day, and his position was excellent. Table Mountain and the Neck barred access to Mirror Valley, and only the tunnel and The Fence offered ingress. In the other direction lay the canyon that opened into Long Valley, and he had no worries about that direction. It was a seventy-mile ride, much of it through the reservation lands, to get to that approach, and the Indians would resent any armed band crossing their lands.

Despite the selfishness of those who would destroy all he had built to save their own cattle, he could feel sympathy for them. He understood what it meant to a cattleman to see his stock dying, yet the water he had would save them for a few days only.

They were clutching at straws, egged on by the hatred of Joe Stangle and by Dulin. Behind it was the leftover hatred for the young Mexican who had married pretty Molly O'Brien, the girl they all wanted.

With cool calculation he began to study his problem.

By noon on Saturday he began work, using a double-jack and a drill. These holes he loaded with powder, determined to blast it shut if need be. It was late afternoon before he completed the work.

From the top of Table Mountain he studied the Mirror Valley country with a field glass his father had given him. He could see the dust clouds that told of moving cattle. No cattle had yet reached Willow Springs, which Candy had told him would be the rendezvous point. Yet by Sunday night he knew the cattle would be massed at the opening of the draw.

Returning to the house he lowered a heavy log gate across the tunnel mouth. Mounting his horse and leading a packhorse, he headed for The Fence.

Once there he studied the terrain with care. The Fence was strong, and his inner fence was stronger. Tearing it out would be no simple job. Climbing the mountain he dug two rifle pits, one forward, the other some distance further back, which he could reach by a hidden route. In each he left ammunition.

No weight of cattle could press down The Fence. It must be torn down or blasted out. Using a crowbar from the packhorse he pried loose a number of boulders and tumbled them down the steep sides of the draw to a place behind The Fence to widen and deepen the barrier.

Further back, where the draw opened into the basin he dug another rifle pit and tumbled down more stones, but there they were more widely spaced and less of an obstruction. Not until darkness had fallen and he could see the dark mass of advancing cattle did he cease work.

Despite the fact that he feared to leave the barricade, he went back to the house and prepared a meal. He was sitting down to eat when he heard a call from the tunnel.

"Merrano?" The shout reached him clearly. "This is Cab Casady! I want to talk!"

Picking up his rifle, his gun belts still hanging from his hips, he walked to the log gate. "What's the problem?" he asked.

The big man grasped the logs. "Merrano, damn it, I'm no talker! I do claim some sense of what's right, and I ain't havin' no part of what they're tryin' to do. I got a rifle here and plenty of shells. I came to lend you a hand!"

"You mean that?" He recalled what Candy had said of this man.

"I sure do, boy! You've got sand, and by the Lord Harry I want to show these bullheads that at least one of us won't be stampeded by no hate-filled coyote like Joe Stangle!"

Barry put down his rifle and unlatched the gate. "Come in, Cab! I won't tell you how good it is to see you!"

The two men walked up to the cabin. Over coffee and side meat Barry explained his defenses. Casady chuckled. "I'll like seein' the expression on Joe Stangle's face when he gets to The Fence!" he said.

They took turns guarding the draw but not until daylight did the cattlemen start to ride up. Barry was at the cabin and he had welcomed another visitor . . . two of them, in fact.

Clyde Mayer, driving his old buckboard, a rifle between his knees, drove up the hill when the gate was opened. Beside him on the seat was Candy Drake. She set her lips stubbornly when she saw Barry.

"If you won't let me shoot I can at least make coffee and get food for you. You'll have to eat."

"All right. I'm not sorry you came. Come on, Mayer, we'd better head back for the draw."

He turned to the girl. "Candy, watch the tunnel. If you hear anybody coming, and you can always hear them, tell them to go away. Fire a couple of warning shots and if they don't leave, light the fuses."

Her features were stiff and white, her eyes large. "I'll do it, Barry. They've no business coming here."

Day was breaking into that gray half-light that precedes the dawn. Cab Casady rose from behind a boulder and came to meet them. "Howdy, Mayer! You joined the army?"

"I have."

Casady was a large, broad-shouldered man with twinkling blue eyes. "They're comin' now," he said. "We better look to it."

"Let me do the talking," Barry suggested. "Maybe we can avoid shooting."

"I doubt it," Cab said. "Stangle wants blood."

When the little cavalcade of riders had approached as far as he thought wise he fired a shot that brought them up standing.

"You boys better ride home. Nobody is coming through the wire, today or ever. I don't want to kill anybody, but I'm protecting my property against armed men."

Casady stood up. "I'm here, too, boys. The first man to touch that wire dies!"

Clyde Mayer called out. "Hill? Is that you? I'm no fighting man, Hill, but by gravy there's going to be some justice in this country! You take my advice and ride home."

"*Mayer?*" Hill's tone was incredulous. "You turned traitor, too?"

"I'm upholding justice, and if you've half the sense I gave you credit for you'll turn around and ride home. I like you, Hill, but you lay a hand on that wire and my bullet will take you right between the eyes!"

There was a hurried conference among the riders. "They can't stop us!" Stangle protested. "They're bluffin'!"

"Count me out," Price Taylor said.

"You yellow?" Dulin sneered.

"You know I'm not yellow," Price Taylor said calmly, "but I've been thinking all the way out here. Merrano whipped me fair and square, and when I was down he didn't put the boots to me but stepped back and let me get up. He made good when we all laughed at him, and he's standing his ground now. As for Mayer, there ain't a fairer, more decent man around than him, and I'll be damned if I'll shoot at him!"

"Then why don't you join him?" Dulin sneered.

Price turned on him. "You called it, Rock! That's just what

I'll do! I've made some bad mistakes and I'm no sky pilot, but I never ganged up on a man with guts. I'll join him!"

He wheeled his horse and started for the barrier. He lifted a hand. "Don't shoot, Merrano! I'm joinin' you!"

Rock Dulin swore viciously and suddenly he whipped up his rifle and fired.

Price Taylor lurched in the saddle, then slipped over on the ground.

"Damn traitor!" Rock Dulin said. "That'll show 'em!"

Tom Drake stared down at the body of Price Taylor. He had reared the boy. He had helped him mount his first horse. He stared around him in shocked bewilderment. "What are we doing?" he said. "Men, what *are* we doing?"

Dropping from his horse he stumbled to the body of Price Taylor.

Jim Hill was white to the lips. Hardy Benson stared after Tom Drake, his face stupid with shock. He looked as if he had awakened from a nightmare. He turned his eyes to Rock Dulin. "That was murder!" he said. "Nothin' but murder!"

Dulin turned like an animal at bay. His eyes went from man to man. "What's the matter? Are you all turnin' yellow? You started out to do it, now you're quittin'!"

Hill sat his horse, his rifle in his hands. "Price Taylor was a good man. He had a right to his feelin's as much as us. Dulin"—his eyes fastened on the other rancher—"you an' Stangle do what you want, but you lift a gun at me, my boys will string you to the nearest cottonwood, an' that's where you belong! We've been a pack of fools, the lot of us!" He turned in the saddle. "Come on, boys, start 'em for home!"

As the Jim Hill hands began gathering the herd, Tom Drake glanced once at the draw, then turned to his own boys. "A couple of you pick up Price," he said.

Lou Barrow looked over at Drake. "Boss, Price was a good man. Too good to get shot in the back."

"I know, but there's been trouble enough today." He walked his horse to where Jim Hill and Hardy Benson sat. "I seem to be gettin' old these days, Jim. I've been lettin' things get out of hand."

"Yeah. Well, this is it, Tom. We're broke."

Silently, the groups scattered, driving their cattle. Dulin spoke to this one or that one but was ignored, cut off, left out of their thinking.

He turned in cold fury to Stangle. "I got a notion to cut the thing myself!"

"Don't try it," Stangle advised. "If he didn't get you, Cab would. We can get even later."

As the three men inside The Fence watched them go, one said, "It will be good to get some warm grub." They turned their horses and rode toward the house.

"Dulin has always been a killer. He shot a man in a gunfight over at Trinidad a few years back," Cab said. "Curt McKesson is another of the same stripe."

Mayer went to his buckboard. "I'll be leaving."

"Watch yourself," Casady advised.

"They daren't bother me," Mayer said. "Without me they can't eat."

Candy was last to go, and Barry rode along with her. At the gate she turned to say good-bye, and he shook his head. "I must talk to your father," he said.

"Do you think that's wise?"

"Maybe not, but he's got a chance to save some of his cattle, if he will listen."

Drake did not look up when they entered. He was seated in his old hide-bound chair, head hanging.

"Father? Here's someone to see you."

He looked up, raising his head like a cornered bear. "Howdy, Merrano. You're lookin' at an old fool."

"Drake"—Barry squatted against the wall—"if you will work to save your herd you can still do it."

"It would have to be soon, boy. They're dyin' like flies."

"Have you been up in the White Hills lately?"

"The White Hills? Not in five or six years. Nothin' up there but pinon an' juniper."

"I think there's water up there," Barry said. "One time down in Texas I saw them bring in an artesian well in country just like that. If you drilled a well just below that old trapper's cabin I think you'd strike water."

"Never heard of any wells drilled in this country," he said doubtfully.

"I've drilled four," Merrano replied, "all with water."

Drake struck a match and held it to his pipe. "Well, it's high time I owned up to thinkin' I was too smart. We old dogs figured we knew all the tricks."

He puffed on his pipe. "Mind if I ride over and have a look at your place? Candy's told me about it."

"You come at any time. As for well-drilling, I've got an outfit I hauled in two years ago from Aragon."

He rode warily on his homeward way. Despite the peaceful discussion with Drake he knew that Stangle and Dulin were still his enemies. The two had ridden off together, and Curt McKesson had ridden with them.

When Tom Drake rode to the basin the next morning, Jim Hill, Vinnie Lake, and Hardy Benson rode with him. They greeted Barry with no more than a nod, and he mounted the steeldust and led them across the basin. Drake pulled in suddenly, pointing to a mound of earth running diagonally across a shallow place on the hill.

"What's the object of that?" he asked.

"Water was starting to make a wash right there," Barry explained, "so I put in that little spreader dam. Causes the water to divide and spread over the hillside and so reaches the roots of more grass.

"Down below where there was a natural hollow, I dug it out a little more with a scraper. Now I've got a pool although it is drying up now."

"More water in that pool right now than I've got on my whole place!" Hill said.

Barry led them from place to place, showing them the lakes he had dammed in the draws, and the various pools. The first of the wells, where he had a windmill pumping, showed a good flow of water. The second, some distance away, was artesian.

The basin looked green and lovely, and he gestured with a wave of the hand. "That's mostly black grama and curly mesquite grass. I let the cattle run there a few weeks, then move them to another pasture and let this grow back. I only run about a third of the stock you have on the same number of acres, that way my stock is always fat."

"My place is all growed up to cholla cactus now," Drake said.

"Burn that field," Barry advised, "the ashes will help the field and the fire will burn the dry needles off the cholla leaving the green pulp behind. That green pulp is fairly good feed. The Navajos taught me that."

"Then I've got enough cholla on my place to feed all the stock in Christendom," Hill said.

"Son," Drake said, "you've done a job! We should have listened to you a long time back."

The days passed swiftly and Barry worked hard, but he was lonely, and even the work failed to help. Each time he returned to the house he kept looking for Candy as he remembered her, making coffee in his kitchen during the fight. At night, alone by the fire, he seemed to see her there. Then one day he rode his horse up the draw and stopped, astonished.

The Fence was gone! Rooted out, wire and posts gone, and the post holes filled in. There might never have been a fence there at all. He pushed his hat back on his head, and shook his head. "Mom," he said aloud, "you'd have liked to see this!"

Candy Drake, riding her pinto, decided to head for the basin. She knew all about The Fence being down. The burning of the cholla had worked and would be the means of saving at least some of the cattle. Now, if the rains came in time or the drillers struck water, they had a fighting chance.

Yet trouble was mounting. Lou Barrow, filled with fury at Rock Dulin's killing of Price Taylor, had gone to town. Barrow had made a remark about killers, and Dulin had gone for his gun. Barrow was a tough cowhand but no gunman, and Dulin put three bullets into him. Miraculously, Barrow lived.

Rock Dulin swaggered about town, his ranch forgotten, his stock dying. Joe Stangle and Curt McKesson were usually with him.

Candy decided it was time the women took a hand. Alice

Benson agreed, and so did the three Lake girls. They organized a big dance and celebration for the purpose of getting everybody together again and wiping out old scores. Candy had taken it upon herself to ride to the basin and invite Barry Merrano.

In other parts of the valley, events were moving in their own way. McKesson had ridden over to Stangle's, and the two sat in the untidy living room over a bottle of whiskey. With nothing on which to feed, Joe Stangle's hatred had turned inward. For days he had been brooding over the thought of Barry Merrano, now the talk of the valley. Joe Stangle's hatred was of long standing, for he had wanted Molly O'Brien and then she had married Miguel Merrano. The fact that Molly had never even noticed his existence made no difference. Deliberately, he provoked trouble with Miguel, confident the Mexican would back down.

The trouble was, he did no such thing. The darkly handsome young Mexican had simply stepped back and told him to go for his gun whenever he was ready.

Suddenly Joe discovered he was not at all ready. It was one thing to tackle what you thought was a puppy dog, quite another when you found yourself facing a wolf with fangs bared. Stangle looked across eight feet of floor and discovered that courage knows no race or creed.

He had backed down, and although it was not mentioned, he knew he was despised for it. His hatred for Miguel Merrano flowered with the coming of his son.

Now, both men were drunk or nearly so. Hulking Curt McKesson reached for the bottle and so did Stangle. Joe got his hand on it as did Curt. In a sudden burst of fury, Stangle jerked the bottle from McKesson's hand.

McKesson's sullen anger, never far from the surface, exploded into rage and he struck with the back of his hand, the blow knocking Stangle sprawling. McKesson was not wearing a gun, having put it aside in the other room.

Joe Stangle, blind with fury, saw nothing but the great hulking figure. All his bottled-up rage found sudden release in this, and his gun slid into his hand, thumbing the trigger again and again.

The thunderous roar of the six-gun filled the room, and with it the acrid smell of gunsmoke. Then the sound died, the smoke slowly cleared, and Joe Stangle lurched to his feet.

One glance at Curt McKesson was enough. The big man was literally riddled with bullets. Averting his eyes, Joe Stangle picked up the bottle and drained off the last of the whiskey. Without a backward glance, he walked out the door.

Drunk as he was his natural cunning warned him he had no chance of getting away with what had been the killing of an unarmed man. Steps were being taken to elect a sheriff and once that was done neither he nor Rock Dulin would long remain at large. Mounting his horse he started down the valley, filled with a sullen feeling that somehow it was all Barry Merrano's fault.

The trail he was riding, drunk, and filled with sullen rage, intersected that of Candy Drake.

Unknown to either of them, Barry Merrano had ridden out of a draw and glimpsed the pinto at a distance. A deep canyon lay between them although they were less than a mile apart, but with luck he could overtake her at Willow Springs.

As he rode he sang a song he had himself composed, a song made up during his loneliness and when he desperately needed something cheerful of which to think.

*"Oh, gather 'round closer and fill up your glasses,*
*And I'll tell you the story of Johnny Go-Day.*
*He was a young cowhand who rode all the mustangs,*
*And no bronco they bred could Johnny dismay!"*

In the cancer of envy that festered in the mind of Joe Stangle was a hatred for all better off or more attractive than himself. Most of all, after Barry Merrano, he hated Candy Drake.

She was a girl who spoke to everyone, but Stangle had

noticed that she did not particularly enjoy speaking to him. He failed to realize this was due to his own surly manner, and the fact that he had been known to make unpleasant remarks about girls and women. He simply believed she thought herself too good for him.

Riding at a canter Candy approached Willow Springs recalling, as she drew near, that her father had told her they had struck water at this, the first well attempted in the valley. Riding up to where the drill rig still stood, she swung down, looking at the pool of muddy water and considering what this could mean to the valley.

It was Barry Merrano's drill rig that had brought in this well, and it was on his advice they had fed the cholla to their stock that saved so much of it. The prejudice against him had virtually disappeared. It could mean a new life for him, and might mean—

She did not hear the horse stop at the edge of the brush. Joe Stangle had seen her arrive, knew she was in there alone, in the gathering dusk. He dug into his saddlebag for the pint he carried there and took a pull at the bottle. He was leaving the country, anyway, and he'd show her what was what. Before anybody knew what had happened he'd be long gone.

He pushed his way through the willows, and Candy turned sharply at the unexpected crackling of the dry brush and saw Joe Stangle.

He was not a big man but he was hairy-chested and broad. His face was swollen and the flesh sodden from much drinking, and he was obviously in an ugly mood.

He had always wanted this girl, and now here she was, with her pride and her stuck-up ways, right in his hands. He started toward her.

Candy realized her danger, but she was not given to screaming. She backed away warily, wishing her horse were closer. If she turned her back to run he would catch her before she had taken three steps.

He did not speak, just walked toward her.

"What's the matter, Joe? Have you lost something?"

He made no reply, continuing to advance. She stepped back

and her boot slipped in the mud and she fell, rolling quickly away and scrambling to her feet.

Drunk he might be, but he could move quickly. "Damn you! You stuck-up—!" She dodged away, but he grabbed at her and caught her wrist. "I'll show you what—!"

In that instant they heard a voice they both knew.

*"Oh, there was a young cowhand who used to go riding,*
*There was a young cowhand named Johnny Go-Day!*
*He rode a black pony and he never was lonely,*
*For the girls never said to him 'Johnny, go 'way!'*
*When they heard his bright laughter their hearts followed after,*
*And they called to him 'Johnny! Oh, Johnny, come stay!'* "

Stangle's hand clamped over the girl's mouth before she could cry out a warning. The pinto stood in plain sight, but Joe Stangle's horse was hidden beyond the brush.

Holding her with one powerful arm and hand, a leg pressed before hers and jamming her back against the drill rig, with his free hand he drew his six-shooter.

The song ended and they heard the saddle creak as he dismounted and then as he started through the willows the song continued.

*"He rode to town daily and always rode gaily,*
*And lifted his hat as he cantered along!"*

Joe Stangle lifted his six-shooter, took careful aim, and squeezed the trigger.

The firing pin clicked on an empty cartridge. He had emptied his gun into Curt McKesson!

At the click of the cocking hammer Barry stopped dead, and with an oath, Joe Stangle threw the girl from him and grabbed feverishly at his cartridge belt for more shells. In his haste he dropped the first two shells but thrust the others into place.

Wild with fear, Candy dropped to the ground and began to scramble away, crying out, "Look out, Barry! It's Joe Stangle!"

Barry grabbed for his gun, still tied down with the rawhide thong he wore when riding. He slid the thong and drew swiftly.

Dropping to one knee, the other leg thrust out before him, he waited. He could hear the breathing of Candy Drake, but in the darkness of the willow grove he could see nothing. Picking up a stick he threw it to one side. Nothing happened.

He moved slightly, gathering himself to leap aside, and at the sound a stab of flame seemed to leap right at his eyes and a bullet struck a tree behind him with an ugly thud. He fired in reply, and his bullet ricocheted off the drill rig.

He fired again, holding a little lower and the shot drew a startled movement. He leaped aside, gun poised for another shot. There was an instant of silence, and then a shot. The bullet missed by a fraction of an inch.

Candy lay hugging the ground, and Barry could see her now. Carefully, he shifted position to get further away from her so as not to draw fire in her direction.

Hatred and fear were driving Joe Stangle, but even the courage of a cornered coyote had a breaking point. The liquor fumes had cleared from his mind, and he realized Barry was over there; he had a gun, and he was playing for keeps.

Suddenly what courage he had went out of him like a gust of breath, and like a shadow, he faded back toward the brush and his horse. He wanted desperately to kill, but he did not wish to be killed. He wanted nothing so much as to get a saddle under him and be off. He almost made it.

Merrano, hearing him at last, lunged through the brush after him. Stangle reached his horse and Merrano slid to a stop, and Joe Stangle saw him and tried one last shot. It was there, and he had to try.

Barry fired at the same instant, then he fired again. Joe Stangle's horse leaped away, and Joe Stangle, shot through the belly, all the hatred oozing away with his life's blood, swayed on his feet, the gun slipping from his fingers. Then he fell.

Barry Merrano turned and started back through the willows and then of a sudden he seemed to step into a hole and he fell.

The clean white bed and the doctor who was putting things

away in a black bag were a surprise. Candy was there, and Cab Casady.

"Stangle?" He started to rise.

"He's gone, Barry. He had already killed Curt McKesson in some kind of drunken fight, and was leaving the country."

"Dulin?"

Cab shifted his feet. "I come by and helped Candy get you home. Then I went down to town and run into Rock Dulin. He picked a fight and I had to shoot him."

Cab started for the door. "You two might have something to talk about," he said. "I want to go watch the rain. Seems like it's years since I've seen any."

# THE ROMANCE OF PIUTE BILL

Tom Galway rode the sorrel out of the juniper and down the hillside toward the rock house on the creek. He was still two hundred yards off and cutting across a field bright with larkspur, paintbrush, and sego lily when he saw Piute Bill come to the door, a Winchester in his hands.

Galway rode up to the door and hooking one leg around the saddle horn he reached for the makings. "You're going to need that rifle, Bill. That is, if you're up to chasing some horse thieves."

"What's happened?" Piute Bill pushed his hat back on his head, then put the Winchester down beside the door. He accepted the tobacco sack Galway handed him. "You losin' stock?"

"Those boys over yonder in the Rubies ran off twenty head of horses last night. I figure to go get 'em."

"All right." Bill touched his tongue to the paper. "Must be eight or nine of them up there. Who do you figure to take along?"

71

"You and me. No use to clutter things up. All I want is somebody to keep them off my back."

"Sure enough. Wait until I saddle up."

He came back from the corral leading a paint horse with one blue eye and one brown eye. Tom Galway was sitting on the porch waiting for him, with a gourd dipper in his hand.

"There's a jug inside," Piute Bill said. "My own make."

Piute Bill threw his saddle on the paint. "Ain't bad whiskey, at that. I'm beginning to think that alkali adds a little bite to her."

"Could be." Galway hefted the jug, then threw it over his bent arm and drank. "Could be," he repeated. "You know, Bill, I'm beginning to think that what you need is a woman. Somebody to sort of cook things up and keep things revved up a mite. Then you could give more time to making whiskey and herding cattle."

Piute Bill glanced at him sourly. "I'm doin' all right. You ready?"

Galway put the jug down inside the door and pulled the door shut. Then he swung into the saddle, and they started off at a walk across the flower-blanketed meadow.

"Cassidy will be there," Piute Bill said, "and Gorman, too." He glanced sidewise at Galway. "You better watch Cassidy. He's a fair hand."

"No man's goin' to run off my stock. I rounded up those horses out on the range. Wild stock. I broke 'em myself and gentled them down. Cassidy's got his business and I have mine. As long as he stays on the other side of the creek, I won't bother him but when he runs off my stock he'd better hunt himself a hole."

The trail led up a shallow gulch bordered by juniper and brush. "You know, Bill," Galway said, "the more I think of you having a woman around, the better I like the idea." He squinted against the sun as they topped out on the rise and looked the country over with care. "Be a sort of a civilizing influence. You ain't getting no younger, and you've been living alone in that shack for some time now. I figure a woman could sort of rev things up around and keep you washed behind the ears."

"You mean," Piute commented sourly, "you figure to drop over time to time for homecooked meals. I know you. I ain't been ridin' the range with you these past four or five years without cuttin' your sign."

"I'm only thinking of you," Galway said, keeping his face straight. "You just think of that schoolmarm over to Summit," Galway continued, ignoring the interruption. "That's a right solid bit of woman, and I hear she's a good cook."

"You'd better be thinkin' of Digger Cassidy. He's no soft touch, and if he stole your horses he wanted them bad. He put lead into Dean Russell over to Battle Mountain, two or three months ago. If you recall, he was one of the roughest of that Charleston outfit."

"Gorman's just as good with a gun."

"There's a slick-ear kid, too. Named Robbins. He shot up a saloon over to Ten Mile last week."

"Heard about him. He files notches on his gun."

"One of them, huh? I never knowed of any real bad man who done that. He's a tinhorn."

The gulch down which they had been riding opened upon a wide, white salt flat and they cut across on an angle, walking their horses to raise no more of the white, smothering dust than necessary. The sky was clear and hot. Their lips became parched and white, their eyes smarted from sweat. Heat waves danced over the flats. They rode in silence, each busy with his own thoughts. The lurking devil in the paint's blue eye went dull with the heat and the slogging pace.

It was two hours before they topped a small rise and left the desert behind them. The sagebrush smelled good after the parched stillness of the salt flats.

Cottonwoods showed some distance off and they pointed their horses, ignoring the trail of the stolen stock, knowing the men they pursued would also need water, and the tracks would begin again when they found it. The horses, smelling water, quickened their pace.

It was a small but cold stream. Men and horses drank. Tom Galway sat down on a rotting tree trunk and scanned the area.

Horses had been held here only a few hours before. Their tracks were in the mud and in the grass.

"About two miles, isn't it? The cabin sets out in the open."

"You got any ideas?"

"I want to talk to Cassidy."

"You want to *talk* to him? Do you reckon he will set around and talk when he knows you're huntin' him?"

Tom Galway was running this show and Piute Bill figured he knew what he was about, but talking to Cassidy at such a time? It didn't make much sense. There had been a good deal of talk about Tom Galway since he had ridden into the Ruby Creek country, and a lot of wondering about him.

"He'll talk," Galway said.

Cassidy and Gorman were known men, both of them had been involved in shootings. With them would be at least six others, all used to fighting for whatever they got. Until now they had confined their raids to the big outfits where weeks might go by before a tally showed that stock was missing. Apparently Tom Galway's stock had been too much of a temptation, and Galway was new in the Ruby Creek country. In the three or four years he had lived there he had kept out of trouble. He had been a hard worker, and obviously a top hand with horses.

Walking to his horse Galway took two strips of rawhide from his saddlebags and tied his gun down to his thigh. Then he took out another gun belt and holster and, after strapping it on, tied it down also. It was the first time Piute had ever seen a man wear two guns, although he had heard of such things.

Piute studied Galway. He was a lean, brown man, tanned by sun and wind. There was a scar over one eye and another along the jawbone. Piute turned his horse and started upstream. Galway cantered until beside him.

"There's timber along the stream," he said, "fifty yards from the cabin. If they open fire we'll take cover there."

Piute couldn't quite make up his mind about Galway. He glanced at the younger man but saw no signs of nervousness or excitement. No more than if he was going after a bunch of cows.

His mind turned to other things. Maybe Galway was right. Maybe he did need a woman. It was lonely there in the cabin in the creek. He was a healthy man, forty years old now, and he had a nice bunch of cattle and a few head of horses. The ranch was doing well, if they didn't start rustling this side of the creek. He figured he could make a wife comfortable, and he wasn't a cantankerous sort.

The creek turned west and they entered the canyon. There was a narrow opening lined with aspen and a few spruce. The trees fell back and the two men cantered over the meadow toward the cabin. It was a squat, stone cabin with a corral almost directly behind it in which Galway could see his horses. Near the stone cabin were three other horses, ground-hitched.

Pulling up about a dozen yards from the door, two men came out, followed by a third and a fourth. The first was Gorman, the second Robbins. The other two Galway did not know. The squat, bull-like figure of Digger Cassidy was nowhere to be seen.

"Howdy," Galway said casually. His eyes scanned their faces and settled on Gorman. "Where's Digger?"

"What d' you want with him?" Robbins demanded belligerently.

"Shut up, Robbins!" Gorman spoke sharply. "I'll do the talking."

He looked at Galway, then at Piute Bill, whose paint had been stopped about ten feet behind and well to the right of Galway. "What do you want?"

"I think Digger made a mistake." Galway spoke gently. "He drove off twenty head of horses for me. Nice meadow here, but I'd rather have them close to home. Thought I'd just ride over and drive them back."

"You thought what?" Robbins' face flushed red. "Just who—!"

"Shut up!" Gorman said impatiently.

There was something here he did not like, and Gorman had pursued a long outlaw career by being cautious. Only two men, and they looked like fighters. Piute Bill he knew about, and he was no man to trifle with.

The other man, a stranger, seemed to be taking the lead, and his quiet, confident manner disturbed Gorman.

"You'll have to talk to Cassidy," Gorman suggested. "He's the boss."

"I know," Galway replied, "but I can't wait. You tell Cassidy that Tom Galway came for his horses. He'll understand."

"You *know* Cassidy?"

"I do. What's more, Digger knows me. You tell him I came for my horses. If he wants me for anything, I'll be at my cabin. Tell him to come whenever he's ready . . . day or night."

He did not turn his head but spoke to Piute. "Kick those corral bars down, Bill. We can't stay long."

Robbins had enough. He stepped forward. "You keep your hands off that corral," he said, "and you, Galway! You get goin' while you're able!"

Gorman was in a quandary. They were four to two. Still, this man said he knew Cassidy, and—

Piute Bill had ignored Robbins. He rode to the corral and leaned toward the bars. Robbins, his face flushed with anger, turned back to Galway. "Stop him! Or I'll kill you!"

Tom Galway's lips smiled, but his eyes did not. "Gorman, this kid's askin' for it."

Robbins' hand streaked for his gun and Galway's sorrel side-stepped suddenly at a touch of the spur. Galway fired . . . then again.

Robbins, his gun half-drawn, stopped dead still, staring at Galway, his eyes blank and unseeing.

Swearing viciously, Gorman went for his gun, trapped into a gun battle he had not wanted. Galway fired, knocking one man into the cabin wall where he fell, knocking the man beside him off balance.

Piute Bill, half behind them, turned at the first shot and fired at Gorman, who went down, his fingers digging into the earth.

The last man dropped his six-shooter as if it were red-hot and flattened against the wall. Galway looked at him over his gun.

The horses were out of the corral and starting toward the bottleneck opening.

Piute Bill's Winchester was ready, and Galway looked at the

last man. "You tell Digger Cassidy to stay on his own side of the creek. Tell him Galway said that, Galway of Tombstone!"

He turned his horse away, watching the man. "And you tell Digger I didn't start the shooting. It was that fool kid, Robbins."

The horses would head for their own corral, now that they were free, but they could always hurry them along a bit.

They were almost out of the bottleneck when a sharp, feminine voice came from the aspens. "All right! Hold up there!"

A buxom, determined-looking young woman of perhaps thirty stepped from the trees. She held a double-barreled shotgun as if she knew how to use it.

Galway and Piute Bill drew up warily. A man with a shotgun was bad enough, but a woman—

"What's the trouble, ma'am?" Galway asked politely. "Can we do something for you?"

"You killed my man back there, and if you think you're gettin' off scot-free, think again!"

Piute Bill started to speak, then swallowed and looked helplessly at Galway.

Lifting his hand slowly, Tom Galway removed his hat. "Now, I'm sorry to hear that, ma'am, but those men stole my horses and when I came after them they made the mistake of trying to shoot it out."

He noted no sign of tears. "Ma'am? Which one was it, Robbins?"

"That puppy?" Contempt was in her tone. "He killed a few tenderfeet and figured he was a tough man. My man was Ned Wavers."

"We're almighty sorry, ma'am," Galway said gently. "We came after our horses. We'd no intention of killing anybody."

"But you did!" There was no grief in her tone, just a hard matter-of-factness. "Ned wasn't much," she said, "but he made me a home, and when he wasn't drunk he took care of me. Now I'll be left here for Cassidy and that bullyin' Tinto Bill."

Tom Galway smiled. "Why, ma'am, if you would rather not stay here, and if it is a home you're looking for, we've got one for you!"

She was, Tom decided, quite a pretty woman. Moreover,

she looked neat, and clean. "Of course," he added, "you'd have to be able to cook."

"There isn't a better cook west of the Pecos," she said flatly, "and I can make pies—"

"Of course," Galway said, smiling, "and we've got just the place for you! It's a pretty little stone house by a creek, and a good, thoughtful man to go with it."

"Hey!" There was sheer panic in Piute's eyes. "Look, you can't—!"

"A good, thoughtful man, ma'am, and a good provider. He's one of the finest hunters around, always has meat for the table."

The shotgun lowered. "What's going on here?" The woman was puzzled. "Somehow, I don't under—"

"Ma'am"—Tom Galway rested his palms, one atop the other, on the saddle horn—"ma'am, this gent with me is Piute Bill. He's a known and respected man. Now he's a mite on the shady side of forty, but steady. He can fork a bronc with any man, one of the best hunters around and he's got him that stone cabin I spoke of.

"It needs a woman's touch, that's all. The right woman. Needs a woman like you, a pretty woman who's neat about the house and who will cook his chuck and keep the place revved up. I know he'd be speakin' for himself, but he's a shy man, not given to talking much."

"Tom! Listen! For God's sake!" His voice trailed off helplessly as Galway continued.

"He makes a little 'shine now and again, but I've never seen him drunk. Don't drink no more than to be sociable. He owns seven hundred head of steers and a milk cow."

"Did you say a milk cow?" The woman looked thoughtful. "If he's got a milk cow he's a sight more of a plannin' man than most. Mister, I reckon you've talked me into it!"

"Mount up, then!" Galway said cheerfully. "Mount up right there behind Piute and put your arms around him and hang on tight. By the time you get to his place on the creek I think he'll be convinced!"

Piute Bill, his eyes vicious and his face red, helped the

young woman up behind him. She flashed a smile at Galway which suddenly faded.

"Now see here! Ned wasn't much and he beat me when he was drunk. I wasn't sorry to lose him, him bein' what he was, but we were all married up, fittin' and proper!"

"Of course, ma'am!" Galway looked shocked. "I'll ride into Ten Mile as soon as I get you to the house. We will have a preacher out here before sundown. The barkeep was tellin' me there was a preacher there now. I'll get him. Meanwhile," he added, "you better just bake a wedding cake. Somehow without a cake a wedding doesn't seem real, does it now?"

"Maybe the preacher won't come?" Bill suggested hopefully.

"He'll come!" Galway said. "I'll see to that!"

"I just bet you will!" Piute said savagely.

Whistling, Tom Galway turned his sorrel toward Ten Mile. "Horse," he said, "I'd make a poor Cupid but sometimes there's things a man just has to do. And besides, she had a scatter-gun."

When Galway rode into Ten Mile the only sign of life was around the Gold Camp Saloon. Galway tied his horse and pushed through the bat-wing doors. There were six men in the place. One sat alone at a table. He was a red-haired man, short and stocky, with a pious look.

Galway stepped to the bar, noticing one of the men was Digger Cassidy, another was Tinto Bill.

"Rye," Galway ordered, and jerking a thumb toward the redhead he asked, "Is that the preacher?"

"It is." The bartender looked up curiously.

"If you've got a horse," he said to the preacher, "better get him saddled. I've got a wedding for you."

"A wedding? Of course, but—?"

"Everything is going to be all legal and proper, this woman wants to marry this man, and by this time," he chuckled, "he'll be wanting to marry her. If she doesn't have him convinced by now she doesn't have the taking ways I think she has. She looked to me like a woman with a mind of her own."

"Who's gettin' married?" the bartender asked.

"Piute Bill. He's been looking for a wife for a long time."

"Who's marryin' him? There ain't more'n three or four single women in the county!"

"Piute Bill," Galway replied carefully, "is marrying Mrs. Ned Wavers."

Tinto Bill choked on his drink. Digger Cassidy turned for the first time and looked right at Tom Galway. "Who?" he demanded, unbelievingly.

"Mrs. Ned Wavers and Piute Bill," Galway repeated. "They are getting married this evening. Soon as I can get the parson up there."

"But she's married!" Tinto Bill said. "She's got a husband, and any time she hasn't, I guess I'd be first in line."

"There must be some mistake," Cassidy said. The light was not good and Galway's hat shaded his face somewhat. "Ned Wavers is—"

"Dead," Galway replied. "Mrs. Ned Wavers has been a widow for almost four hours."

Digger Cassidy spoke softly. "You say Ned Wavers is dead."

"That's right, Digger. Seems some of your boys drove off some horses of mine last night, so I rode over to drive them back. Robbins made a fool play and Gorman and Wavers tried to back him up."

Silence filled the room. The preacher swallowed, and the sound was loud in the room.

"Mrs. Wavers didn't want to be left behind and as she kind of hit it off with Bill they decided to get married."

He was watching Cassidy, and a few feet to one side, Tinto Bill. "By the way, Cassidy, I told that other fellow, the one who's alive, to suggest you keep to your side of the creek and I'd keep to mine. I went to a good deal of trouble to catch and train those horses, and I don't want to lose them."

Neither Cassidy nor Tinto Bill had moved. Without turning his attention from them, Galway said, "Rev'rend, get your horse. I'll be with you in a minute."

The preacher vanished through the door.

Cassidy spoke suddenly. "You can't get away with this! I don't care if you are Galway of Tombstone!"

"Take it easy. If we shoot it out now, I'll kill you. Maybe

you'd get me, but that wouldn't help you any. You'd be just as dead, and I never missed nobody at this range."

"Why should you get killed over horses you didn't have no business stealin' and a woman who's obviously been living a dog's life?"

"I didn't steal your damn horses!" Cassidy said. "It was that fool Robbins!"

"I can believe that," Galway agreed. "In fact, I'd of bet money on it. So why should we shoot it out? It makes no sense. Now I'm going to leave. I've got to get that preacher back up on the mountain because that's a decent woman yonder."

"Damn it, Galway!" Cassidy protested. "Why couldn't you have come when I was to home? Once I knew those were your horses I'd have driven them back!"

"All right," Galway said, "I'll take your word for it." Deliberately he started to turn his back and when he did, Tinto Bill went for his gun.

Galway palmed his gun and shot across the flat of his stomach. Tinto, his gun up, fired into the ceiling, took two slow steps and fell on his face, his gun skidding along the floor.

Digger Cassidy stood very carefully near the bar, his hands in plain sight.

"Looks to me, Digger," Galway said, "like you're fresh out of men. Why don't you try Montana?"

He turned abruptly and walked out.

Digger Cassidy moved to the bar and took up the drink the bartender poured for him. "Damn him!" he said. "Damn him to hell, but he can sure handle a gun!"

He downed his drink. "Bartender," he said, "if you ever go on the road, steer clear of hotheaded kids who think they are tough!"

Tom Galway rode up to the stone cabin with a saddle-sore preacher just after sundown. Piute Bill, in a clean shirt and a fresh shave, was seated by the fireplace with a newspaper; from the stove came a rattle of pans.

The future Mrs. Piute Bill turned from the stove. "You boys light an' set. It surely isn't right to have a wedding without a cake!"

"I couldn't agree with you more, ma'am!" Galway said. "Nobody likes good cooking more than me."

Piute Bill stared at Galway, the venom in his eyes fading under a glint of humor. "You durned catamount! You durned connivin' Irish son-of-a- . . ."

"Ssh!" Tom Galway whispered. "There's a preacher present!"

# HATTAN'S CASTLE

Hattan's Castle, a towering pinnacle of rock that points an arresting finger at the sky, looks down on a solitary frame building with a sagging roof, a ruined adobe, and several weed-covered foundations, all that is left of a town that once aspired to be a city.

On a low mound a quarter of a mile away are three marked graves and seventy-two unmarked, although before their wooden crosses rotted away a dozen others had carried the names and dates of pioneers.

East of the ruined adobe lies a long and wide stone foundation. Around it there is a litter of broken bottles and a scattered few that the sun has turned into collector's items. Twenty feet behind the foundation, lying among the concealing debris of a pack-rat's nest, is a whitened skull. In the exact center of that skull are two round holes less than a half-inch apart.

Several years ago the scattered bones of the skeleton could still be seen, but time, rain, and coyotes being what they are, only the skull remains.

Among the scattered foundations are occasional charred timbers, half-burned planks, and other evidences of an ancient fire. Of the once booming town of Hattan's Castle nothing more remains.

In 1874, a prospector known as Shorty Becker drank a stolen bottle of whiskey on the spot. Drunk, he staggered to the edge of the nearby wash and fell over. Grabbing for a handhold he pulled loose a clump of manzanita and the town of Hattan's Castle was born.

Under the roots and clinging to the roots were flecks and bits of gold, and Shorty Becker, suddenly sober, filed on one of the richest claims in the state's history.

Nineteen other lucky gentlemen followed, and then a number who were only fairly lucky. Hattan's Castle went from nothing to a population of four thousand people in seven days, and three thousand of the four came to lie, cheat, steal, and kill each other and the remaining one thousand odd citizens, if such they might be called.

Spawned from an explosive sink of sin and evil, the town lived in anarchy before the coming of John Daniel. When he arrived the town had found its master. With him were the hulking Bernie Lee and a vicious little murderer who called himself Russ Chito.

Marshal Dave Allen went out in a burst of gunfire when he had words with John Daniel. Daniel faced him but fired only one shot, the others were fired by Russ Chito and Bernie Lee, in ambush on opposite sides of the street and taking the marshal in a deadly cross fire.

Shorty Becker was found dead two days later, a gun in his hand and a bullet in his brain. John Daniel, a self-appointed coroner, pronounced it suicide. Becker was found to be carrying a will naming Daniel as his only friend and heir.

Daniel turned the working of the mine over to others, and opened the Palace Saloon & Gambling Hall. From the Barbary Coast he imported some women and a pair of bartenders skilled in the application of mickeys, knockout drops, or whatever most suited the occasion.

Four years passed and Hattan's Castle boomed in lust, sin, and murder. The mines continued to prosper, but the miners and owners remained to spend, to drink, and to die. The few who hoarded their gold and attempted to leave were usually found dead along the trails. Buzzards marked their going and if a body was found it was buried with the usual sanctimonious comments and some hurry, depending on the condition of the remains. John Daniel, aloof, cold, and supercilious, ruled the town with a rod of iron.

Chito and Lee were at his right hand but there were fifty others ready to do his bidding. Immaculate always, coldly handsome and deadly as a rattler, John Daniel had an air of authority which was questioned by none. Of the seventy-five graves on boot hill at least twenty had been put there by him or his henchmen. That number is conservative, and of those found along the trail at least half could be credited to John Daniel's cohorts. Then Bon Caddo came to town.

He was Welsh by ancestry, but what more he was or where he had come from nobody ever knew. He arrived on a Sunday, a huge man with broad, thick shoulders and big hands. His jaw was wide and hard as iron, his eyes a chill gray and calm, his head topped with a wiry mass of rust-colored hair. The claim he staked four miles from the Castle was gold from the grass roots down.

Within two hours after the strike Russ Chito dropped in at the Palace. John Daniel stood at the end of the bar with a glass of sherry.

"Boss," Chito said, "that new feller in town struck it rich up Lonetree."

"How rich?"

"They say twenty thousand to the ton. The richest ever!"

John Daniel mentally discounted it by half, possibly even less. Even so it made it extremely rich. He felt his pulses jump with the realization that this could be what he was waiting for, to have enough to be free of all this, to buy a home on Nob Hill and live the life of a gentleman, with no more Russ Chitos to deal with.

"Invite him in. Tell him I want to see him."

"I did tell him, and he told me where I could go." Russ Chito's eyes flickered with anger. "I'd like to kill the dirty son!"

"Wait. I want to talk to him."

Bon Caddo did not come to Hattan's Castle and his gold did not leave the country. Every stage, every wagon, and every rider was checked with care. Nothing left the country but Bon Caddo continued to work steadily and hard, minding his own affairs, uninterested in the fleshpots of the Castle. He was cold to all offers from John Daniel, and merely attended to business. Efforts to approach him were equally unsuccessful, and riders always found themselves warned away by an unseen voice and a rifle that offered no alternative.

At the beginning of the third month, John Daniel called Cherry Creslin to his office. She came at once, slim, beautifully curved and seductive in her strictly professional way.

"You like to ride," Daniel said, "so put on that gray habit and ride my black. How you do it is your own affair, but get acquainted with Bon Caddo. Make him like you."

She protested. "Sorry, John. Get one of the other girls. I want no part of these drunken, dirty miners."

"You'll do as I tell you, Cherry, and you'll do it now. This man is neither drunken nor dirty. He is big, and tough, and, I think, dangerous. Also, he cares nothing for gambling or whiskey."

She got up. "All right, I'll go. But you'll wish you'd never sent me. I'm sick of these jobs, John! Why don't we cash in our chips and pull out? Let's go to New York, or San Francisco."

"Get started. I'll tell you when to go, and where."

The canyon of the Lonetree was warm in the spring sunshine. The cottonwoods whispered secrets to each other above the stream that chuckled humorously to the stones. There was no other sound but the trilling of birds, and on the bank above the stream the sound of Caddo working.

He wore a six-shooter, and a rifle stood nearby, and just out of sight in the tunnel mouth was a shotgun, a revolving weapon made by Colt.

Standing with his feet wide apart in their heavy miner's boots, he made a colossal figure. He was freshly shaved, and his shock of rusty hair was combed. His red flannel shirt was open at the neck, and his huge forearms, bulging with raw power, showed below his rolled-up sleeves. Cherry Creslin, impressed by few things, was awed.

At the sound of hooves splashing in the water, he looked around. Then he saw the rider was a woman, and a beautiful woman, at that. He smiled.

Long before he had come to Hattan's Castle he had heard of John Daniel, and knew his every trick. Moreover, he knew this woman by name and knew she was reputed to be John Daniel's own woman. He could see, as she drew nearer, that she was genuinely beautiful and despite the hard lines that showed through her lovely skin, there was warmth there, but a restrained, carefully controlled warmth.

"Good morning, Bon Caddo." Her voice was low and lovely, and deep within him something stirred, and he tried to bring up defenses against it. She was all woman, this one, no matter what else she might be.

"Hello, Cherry."

"You know me? I don't remember you." She looked at him again. "I don't think I could forget."

"You've never seen me, Cherry, and I've never seen you, but I've been expecting you."

He gestured to a seat under a tree. "Won't you get down and stay for a while? It's quite pleasant here."

"You—you've been expecting me?" She was irritated. She was accustomed to handling men, to controlling situations. This man, she realized, was different. Not only was he a physical giant but he was intelligent, and . . . she admitted it reluctantly . . . he was exciting.

"Of course." He smiled pleasantly. He had, she thought, a truly beautiful smile. "John Daniel has tried everything else, hasn't he? Everything but you . . . and murder."

Her features stiffened and her eyes went hard, but she did not pretend to misunderstand. "So you think he sent me? You think I am the kind of woman a man can send on some dirty business?"

He leaned on his shovel. "Yes," he said, and she struck him across the face with her quirt.

He did not move nor change expression although the red line of the blow lay vividly across his cheek and lips. "Yes," he repeated, "but you shouldn't be. You've got heart and you have courage. You've just been riding with the tide."

"You're very clever, aren't you?"

"No. But this situation isn't very hard to understand. Nor are you, Cherry Creslin. It's a pity," he continued, "that you're tied up with such a murdering lot. There's a lot of woman in you, and you'd make some man a woman worth keeping."

She stared at him. The situation was out of hand. It would be difficult now to get him back in the right vein. Or was this the right one?

"You may be right," she said, "maybe I've been waiting for you."

He laughed and stuck his shovel down hard into the pile of muck. Then he walked over to her, and the black horse nuzzled his arm. "Not that way, Cherry. Be honest. I'm not so easy, you know. Actually the only way is to be honest."

She measured him, searching herself. "Honest? I don't know whether I could be. It's been so long."

"Ah, now you are being honest! I like that, Cherry." He leaned his big shoulder against the horse's shoulder. "In fact, Cherry, I like you."

"Like me?" A strange emotion was rising within her, and she tried to fight it down. "And you know what I am?"

"What are you? A woman. Perhaps no worse and no better than any other. One cannot always measure by what a person seems to be or even has been. Anyway, it is always the future that counts."

"You believe that? But what of a woman's past?"

Bon Caddo shrugged. "If a woman loved me I'd start counting the days of her life from the time she told me she loved me. I would judge by what happened after that, although I'd be a hard judge for the after years."

She was irritated with herself. This was not what she had come for. "How did we start talking like this? I did not intend to get into anything like this."

"Of course. You came to get me to fall in love with you or at least to lure me down to that sinkhole at Hattan's Castle. You might manage the first, but not the last."

"If you were in love with me and I asked you to come, would you?"

"Certainly not. Doing what a woman asks is not proof of love. If a man isn't his own man he isn't worthy of love. No, I'd use my own judgment, and my judgment tells me to stay away from Hattan's Castle and the Palace."

His eyes seemed to darken with seriousness. "We of Welsh or Irish blood, Cherry, sometimes have a power of prophecy or intuition, call it what you will, and mine tells me that when I come to Hattan's Castle it will mean blazing hell and death. For me, the town, or both of us."

Something cold and frightening touched her and suddenly she put her hand on his. "Then, then don't come, Bon Caddo. Don't come at all. Stay here, or better still, take your gold and go."

"You advise me that way? What would John Daniel say?"

"He wouldn't like it," she replied simply. "He would not like it at all. But it is my best advice to you."

"I shall stay until my claim is worked out. I'll not be driven off."

"May I come back again?"

"Come soon. Come often."

Caddo watched her go and then returned to his work. There would be trouble, of course. He doubted that Cherry would tell John Daniel of her failure. Not yet, at least. She would come back, and perhaps again. If she continued to fail, John Daniel would try something else.

Three times she came in the days that followed and each time they talked longer. Inevitably the day came when she returned to Hattan's Castle to find John Daniel awaiting her. When their eyes met she knew she was in trouble.

"Well?" His question was a challenge. "When is he coming in?"

"He is not coming at all." There was no use evading the issue. She had probably been spied upon. "He is not coming, but I am leaving. We're to be married."

"*What?*" Of all things, this was the least expected. "Do you think you can trick me that way? Marry him and get it all for yourself?"

"You'd not understand, John, but I love him. He's a real man and a fine man, so don't try to stop me."

"Try? I'll not just try, I'll do it!" His eyes were ugly. "Hereafter you will stay in town. I shall find other means of handling it."

"Sorry." She got to her feet. "I am going back to him."

He struck her across the mouth with the back of his hand and she fell to the floor, a trickle of blood running from her mashed lip. She looked up at him. "You shouldn't have done that, John. I am sorry for you, or I would be if there was a decent bone in your body."

Furious, he strode from the room and returned to the Palace. The first person he saw was Chito. "All right. You want to kill Caddo. Go do it."

Without another word, Russ Chito left the room. From her window Cherry saw him go and divined his purpose. Filled with terror she rushed to the door but hulking Bernie Lee stood there. "You ain't goin' no place. Get back inside."

She stepped back. There would be no chance to warn Caddo. Chito would be halfway there by now, and he would kill without warning, and from ambush.

At the Palace John Daniel stared from the window, thinking. The boom was over here, anyway. He would sell out and go away. Within the past few months the population had fallen by a third. It was time to move. With the gold from Caddo's claim he could leave all this behind. He would go to San Francisco as they had planned, and he would take Cherry with him. Once away from all this the foolish notions would leave her head. She would be his woman again.

During the months they had been associated he had never

won her love, and it galled him to think that Bon Caddo had, or so it seemed.

John Daniel hated all that resisted him; anything he did not or could not possess and control.

The afternoon wore on, and he paced the floor. Chito had not returned. Of course, he was a careful man. He was taking his time. Still—

In her own cabin, Cherry packed her belongings and waited. She feared, she doubted, yet inside there was a kind of stillness. Terror there was, and fear for the man she now loved, but through it all there was something else, a kind of confidence, a belief that somehow, some way, Bon Caddo would triumph.

At the Palace Saloon John Daniel was no longer patient. He lit a black cigar and muttered under his breath. He walked to the door and looked down the street. There was no sign of Chito.

Darkness came and he went to his office. The saloon business began but in a desultory fashion. The whole town seemed to be waiting, watching, wondering. Seven o'clock passed, then eight. John Daniel walked into the saloon and looked quickly around. Many of the familiar faces were missing. Nine came and went and suddenly there was a crash of glass. Men sprang to their feet, staring.

Where the alley window had been was a gaping hole, and sprawled on the floor inside was Russ Chito. He had taken a shotgun blast through the chest.

Men rushed to him, and only John Daniel remained where he was, white-faced, his cigar clamped in his teeth.

Then the swinging doors parted and Bernie Lee tottered into the room and fell sprawling on the floor. He was alive, but brutally beaten.

John Daniel reached behind the bar and took up a spare pistol. Methodically, he checked it, then tucked it behind his belt. His own gun in his hand, he strode down the street.

Cherry was gone.

Her house was lighted, the door stood open, but Cherry was gone.

John Daniel swore, shifted the cigar in his teeth. "Pete! Dave! Ed! Cherry's gone and I want her back, and I want Bon Caddo dead!'"

Suddenly, from down the street a voice shouted *"Fire!"* John Daniel rushed to the door. One glimpse was enough, down the street, in a direct line with his saloon, a deserted shack was ablaze.

A glance told him that with the wind there was no chance. That whole side of the street must go, and he owned every building there.

Suddenly he became aware that nobody was moving to fight the blaze. They were watching, and a few were throwing water on buildings across the street, buildings he did not own. He yelled at them, but there was no response.

Cursing, he turned on his heel and went into the Palace. Rage filled him, a bitter, futile rage. He was whipped . . . whipped. But he still had the money.

He went to his secret drawer and took out the gold. He went to his safe for more, carefully changed into bills for easier carrying. There was more gold under the foundation but that could wait. Now, while the others watched the fire, he would go.

From his room he brought a pair of saddlebags, kept handy for the purpose, and into them he stuffed bills and gold. Straightening up he turned swiftly and started for the back door. A few steps beyond was the stable and his black horse.

He stopped abruptly. Bon Caddo stood in the door. "Going some place, John?" he asked mildly.

John Daniel stood stock-still, caught in midstride. For the first time he knew fear.

He was alone. Russ Chito was dead. Bernie Lee was beaten within an inch of his life. The others were scattered, hunting for Caddo. And Caddo was here.

John Daniel had always accounted himself a brave man. He was not afraid, but there was something indomitable about Caddo.

"All your life, John Daniel, you've lived by murder and

robbery, and you've gotten away with it. Now your town is burning, Daniel, and you're going with it."

John Daniel's hand reached for a bottle at the end of the bar and threw it. The bottle missed, shattering against the wall. Bon Caddo started for him.

John Daniel moved to meet him, since there was no escape. He struck out viciously, and Caddo took the blow coming in without so much as a wince. Then Caddo struck in return, and the blow made Daniel's knees buckle.

Caddo moved after him, coolly, relentlessly. "Like hitting women, John? How does it feel to be hit? Do you like killing, John? How does it feel to die?"

In a wild burst of panic-born strength, John Daniel struck out. The blow caught Caddo coming in again but the power of it staggered him and he tripped over a fallen chair, falling to the floor.

John Daniel lunged for the back door and made it. With Caddo coming after him he reached the stable.

His horse was gone!

Trapped, he turned swiftly, reaching for his gun. In front of Bon Caddo a red eye winked, then winked again. Thunder roared in John Daniel's ears and a terrible flame seemed to rush through him. He did not see the red eye wink again for he was falling, falling, already dead, into the broken branches of a manzanita.

There is a place in the Tonto Basin where a long, low ranch house looks out upon a valley. Cottonwood leaves whisper their secrets around the house and on the veranda a woman watches her husband walking up from the barn with his two tall sons. Inside the house a daughter sings songs more haunting than those her mother sang in the Palace, long ago. The big man, whose hair is no longer rust red, pauses by her side.

Before them, the peace of the meadows, and the tall sons washing for supper in the doorside basins. Inside, the song continues.

"It's been a good life, Mother, a good life," he says quietly.

Far to the north there is an adobe wall with a bullet buried in it, a bullet nobody ever saw. A smashed elbow bone, covered now by the sand of the wash, lies among the debris of a pack-rat's nest, and where the manzanita grew there is a whitened skull. In the exact center of that skull are two round bullet holes, less than a half inch apart.

# DUFFY'S MAN

Duffy's man had been on the job just six days when trouble started.

Duffy, who was older than the gnarled pin-oak by the water hole, knew there would be trouble when he saw Clip Hart riding up to the stable. Duffy had covered a lot of miles in his time, and had forgotten nothing, man or animal, that he had seen in his travels.

Clip Hart had killed a man seven years before in El Paso, and Duffy had seen it happen. Since then there had been other killings in other towns, and three years in the state pen for rustling. From time to time Hart had been investigated in connection with robberies of one kind or another.

Hart was older, heavier, and harder now. He had the coldly watchful eye of a hunted man. There were two men with him and one of them rode across the street to the Pine Saloon and stood alongside his horse, watching the street.

Hart looked at the sign on the livery stable and then at the

95

fat old man in the big chair. "You're Duffy?" Hart measured him as he spoke.

"I'm Duffy." The old man shifted his bulk in the polished chair. "What can I do for you?"

"The use of your stable. I've seven horses coming in tonight. They'll be kept here in your stable, saddled all the time."

Duffy shifted himself in his seat. "None of that here. I'll not want your business. Not here."

"You'll keep them. You don't move very fast, Duffy." Clip Hart struck a match on the seat of his pants and held up the flame. "Your barn can't move at all." He lifted the flame suggestively. "Where's your hostler?"

Duffy turned his head on his fat neck. He was no fool, and he knew Hart was not bluffing. He opened his mouth to call for his hostler, and as he turned his head he saw him there, standing in the door, his hands on his hips.

Duffy's man was tall, lean, and wide-shouldered. His face was still. Sometimes his eyes smiled, rarely his lips. The stubble of beard he had worn when Duffy hired him was gone now, but he wore no hat and he still wore the worn, badly scuffed shoes, unusual foot gear in a country of boots and spurs.

There was a small scar on one cheekbone and sometime long ago his nose had been broken. He was probably twenty-five but he looked older, and the years behind him had probably been rugged years.

Clip Hart stared at him. "There'll be seven horses brought here tonight. Keep them saddled and ready to go. Understand?"

Duffy's man jerked a thumb at Duffy. "I take my orders from him."

Hart's anger flared. He was a man who could not accept resistance of any kind. It drove him to a killing fury and Duffy knew it, and was worried. "You'll take my orders!" Hart said. "Get back inside!"

Deliberately, the hostler glanced at Duffy and the old man nodded. Duffy's man turned on his heel and went back inside.

"You'll get paid, and plenty," Hart was telling Duffy, "but no arguments, understand?" Then, his tone thick with contempt, he added, "Who in this town could make trouble for us?"

When Hart crossed the street to the saloon, Duffy's man returned to the door. "You goin' to take that?"

"We've no choice. I'm no gunslinger. There's no more than seven men in town right now, all quiet, peaceful men. Anyway, their womenfolks would be scared. We've been expectin' something of the kind for a long time." He looked around. "You're new here. Those men are bad, real bad."

Duffy's man merely looked at him. "Are they?" he asked.

He walked back into the stable and climbed to the loft, forking hay into the mangers, then put corn into seven feed boxes. Walking out he said, "I'll eat now," slipping into his coat as he spoke. He did not look at Duffy. The three horses were still across the street.

There was a sign that said MA'S KITCHEN and when he went inside there were two tables eight feet long with a bench along each side and at each end. Clip Hart was sitting at the end of one table with his back to the wall. Duffy's man sat down alongside the table near the opposite end.

He had been born in the West but left with his mother when he was ten and had grown up in the streets of New York. At fifteen, after two years working on a fishing boat he had shipped out around the Horn. He dealt monte in a Barbary Coast dive, fought a series of bareknuckle fights, and won them. He had become friendly with Jem Mace and learned a lot about fighting from him, the master boxer of his time. At seventeen he was on a windjammer in the China Sea. Back in New York again he fought several more bareknuckle fights and won each time.

Discontented with his life he found an interest in books and began to study with an eye to bettering himself, although without any definite idea. Running out of money he worked his way West on the railroad and finally, dead broke, he dropped off the stage in Westwater.

Westwater had one restaurant, one saloon, a livery stable, a blacksmith shop, a crossroads store, and a stage station which doubled as a post office.

Julie came around the table and put a plate before him. He thanked her and watched her fill the cup. She was a slender girl with Irish blue eyes, black hair, and a few freckles. She left him and went around the table, picking up several dirty dishes. It looked like at least three men had left without finishing their meals when Hart came in.

"More coffee!" Hart looked at the girl as he spoke, boldly appraising. When she went to fill his cup he slipped an arm around her waist.

She stepped away so quickly that it jerked Hart off balance and his face turned ugly with anger.

"Put that pot down and come here!" he said.

"Keep your hands to yourself!" Julie flared. "I'll serve you, but I won't be pawed by you!"

Clip started to rise but Duffy's man grabbed the table and shoved hard. The end of the table hit Hart's hip as he was turning to rise, and it caught him off balance. He staggered, the bench behind tripped him. He fell hard, his feet flying up.

Duffy's man stood over him. "Let her alone," he said. "A man in your business can't afford to fool around."

"You're tellin' me my business?" He gathered his feet under him but he was in no position to argue, and something in the face of Duffy's man warned him.

At the same time he realized that what the hostler said was true. He could not afford trouble here and now. He could wait. He got carefully to his feet. "Aw, I was just foolin'!" he said. "No need for her to be so persnickety."

Then as he started to brush himself off, his anger flared again. "You shoved that table!" he exclaimed.

"You catch on fast." Duffy's man spoke calmly, standing there with his hands on his hips, just looking at Hart. The outlaw grew more and more angry. At the same time he felt an impulse to caution. No trouble here and now. That could wait.

Without another word he drew back his bench and sat down. When he had finished eating he threw a half-dollar on the table and went out without so much as a backward glance.

Julie filled his cup again. "He won't forget that."

"I know."

"He'll kill you. He's killed other men."

"Maybe."

Duffy's man finished his meal in silence, ever conscious of her presence. When he got up he dropped two bits on the table to pay for the meal, then went to the door. "You be careful," she warned.

He crossed the street and saw the horses the men had ridden into town were gone. It was dark now, but he could still see Duffy seated in his big old chair.

"Horses come?"

"Not yet." Duffy's chair creaked. "What happened over there?"

"He got fresh with Julie, and I shoved him down with a table. He didn't like it very much."

"He'll kill you."

"I'm not ready to die."

"Take a horse," Duffy advised. "Take that little bay. If you ever get the money you can send it to me. If not, forget it. I like you, son."

"I don't need a horse."

"You won't have a chance."

"You go home, Mr. Duffy, and don't come out tomorrow. Leave this to me. It's my fight."

Duffy's chair creaked as he got up. "The bay's in the box stall if you want it." He paused near the corner of the barn. "Have you got a gun?"

"No, I don't think I'll need one." He was silent, and he was aware that the old man had not moved, but stood there in the shadows.

"The way I see it," he said, "they've got this town treed. They can do as they please. First they will use it as a way station for fresh horses, then they'll take over the town's business, then the people. Men will be killed and women taken."

"Maybe."

"You go home now, Mr. Duffy. You stay out of this."

Duffy's man listened to the slow, retreating steps. Duffy must be nearly eighty. The storekeeper was well past sixty. The tough young men of the town were all gone on a cattle drive. They would be back next year, or maybe they would never come back. The hardships of a cattle drive being what they were. It made no difference now. He was a man who knew what had to be done and he was not accustomed to asking for help.

He sat down in Duffy's chair and waited. There had been a man in a railroad construction camp who was always quoting, and those quotations had a way of sticking in the mind. Duffy's man stirred in the chair, remembering one the fellow had loved to quote. Time and again he had said it.

> They tell us, Sir, that we are weak, unable to cope with so formidable an adversary. But when shall we be stronger? Will it be next week? Will it be next year? Will it be when we are totally disarmed and a guard stationed in every house? Shall we gather strength by irresolution and inaction? Sir, we are not weak if we make proper use of those means which the God of nature has placed in our power.

The words had a nice sound and he said them aloud, but softly, listening to the smooth sound of them on his lips. He had the Irishman's love of fine sounding words and the Irishman's aptitude for rebellion. He leaned back in the chair and closed his eyes. The fellow in the construction camp who quoted that, he had been better than a book, and all he needed to start him off was a bit of rye whiskey.

It was past midnight when the horses came. Two riders led them up under the trees and then across the street to the stable. One man remained outside in Duffy's chair while the other helped Duffy's man tie them in the stalls. They were all fine, beautifully built animals.

The man was stocky and not very tall. He lifted the lantern to the hostler's face. "New?"

"Drifting."

"You take good care these horses are ready. You do that and you'll have no trouble. You might even find a few extra bucks in your kick when this is over. Do you hear me?"

"I hear you."

The man walked back to the door but did not step out into the light. There was a lantern over the door that was kept burning all night, and it threw a pale glow around the stable door.

Duffy's man watched the glow of their cigarettes and then he went to the harness room. There were several old saddles, odds and ends of harness, and in a corner, behind a dusty slicker there was something else.

It was a Colt revolving shotgun.

He peered out a crack of the door, then put the lantern on the floor between himself and the door. Taking up the shotgun he wiped it free of dust, then he took it apart and went to work on it.

Several times he went to the door to peer out. After almost two hours of work he had the shotgun in firing condition. The cylinder would no longer revolve of itself but could be turned by hand. Duffy's man fed shells into the four chambers. They were old brass shotgun shells, and he had loaded them himself. Then he stood the shotgun back in the corner and hung the slicker over it.

The short, stocky man was in the chair now and the other one was asleep on the hay just inside the door. Duffy's man stopped inside the door. "What time tomorrow?" he asked.

The fellow looked around at him. "Maybe noon. Why?"

"Wonderin' if I should feed them again. They won't run good on a full stomach."

"Say, that's right. Feed 'em now, I s'pose. All right?"

"Yeah."

Duffy's man walked back inside and fed the horses. "They tell us, sir, that we are weak," he repeated, "but when shall we be stronger?"

He thought it over as he stood there, rubbing the sorrel's neck. "It has a nice sound," he told the horse, "a nice sound."

He walked to the door. "Soon be daylight," he said, "the sky's turning gray."

"Yeah." The stocky man got to his feet and stretched. Duffy's man hit him.

It was a backhand blow with his left fist that caught the stretching outlaw in the solar plexus. Duffy's man stepped around in front of him and with the practiced ease of the skilled boxer he uppercut with the left and crossed a right to the chin. The outlaw never had a chance to know what was happening, and the only sound was a gasp at the backhand to the solar plexus.

Duffy's man pulled him out of sight behind the door. Then he tied his hands and feet and stuffed a dirty rag into his mouth for a gag, tying it there.

Leaning over the sleeping outlaw he very gently lifted the man's hand and slipped a loop over it. His eyes flared open but the hostler grasped his upper arm and flipped him over on his face before he realized what was happening.

Shoving the man's face into the hay and earth, he dropped on one knee on the man's back and jerked his other wrist over to receive a second loop. Quickly, with a sailor's skill with knots, he drew the wrists together and bound them tight, then tied his feet and gagged him.

They might, he thought, get themselves free just when he was most busy. He dragged them to the center of the barn where there was no loft. It was almost forty feet to the ridgepole. Climbing the ladder to the loft he then mounted a ladder that led to the roof and rigged two ropes over a crosspiece, then went back to the floor.

The outlaws, both conscious now, stared at him, horrified.

"Going to hang you," he said cheerfully, grinning at their agonized expressions. "But not by the necks . . . unless you struggle."

Twenty minutes later he looked up at them with appreciation. More than thirty feet above the hard packed earth of the barn floor he had suspended the two outlaws. Each man had a loose noose around his neck. If they struggled to get free and the knots started to slip they would hang themselves.

"It's up to you," he explained. "You can hang there quietly and when this shindig is over I'll let you down easy. You struggle and you'll both be dead."

He strolled to the door. Smoke was lifting from Ma's Kitchen and Julie was sweeping off the step. He walked across and she glanced up, smiling at him. He saw her eyes go past him to the barn door. The chair was empty.

She got the coffeepot and filled his cup, stealing a glance at his face, which revealed nothing. She had heard the riders come in with the horses, and she knew it meant a bank holdup somewhere near.

The outlaws could run their horses at top speed, switch to fresh horses and be off to the mountains. The fresh horses would assure them of escape, for any posse would have to run their horses hard to try to catch them, and those horses would have been extended to the utmost before reaching Westwater.

Duffy's man ate in silence. When he arose he dropped a quarter on the table. "Better stay inside today," he told Julie, "and tell Ma."

She stopped at the end of the table. "Whatever it is you're planning," she said, "don't do it. You don't know Clip Hart."

"There are Clip Harts wherever one goes. If you start running there's no place to stop. I have it to do or I have to run, and I don't run easy.

"Anyway"—he spoke in a lighter tone, not looking at her—"a man has to stop somewhere and make a start. This seems as good a place as any. A man might even start a ranch of his own."

"That takes money."

"A man who is good with an ax might make some money cutting ties for that branch line they're about to build. They will need ties," he added, "or they'll have to ship them a long way."

He went out without looking back, but he heard Ma say, "I like that young man."

Julie answered, "He won't live long if he bucks Clip Hart."

At the foot of the steps Duffy's man stopped, thinking. How did one man handle seven men? And how far behind the outlaws would the posse be? How long would it take them to get to Westwater?

Duffy's man considered a half dozen ways of delaying the outlaws and still staying alive. Tying their horses with hard knots? They would cut the ropes. Opening fire as they entered the street? He didn't have shells enough to kill them all if he scored with every shot, and they were too many. He would himself be dead.

There was no way. He had been foolish to begin what he could not end, and he was very glad he had not tried to enlist help in his foolhardy scheme. It had been all too easy to think of doing something, all too easy to say they would never be stronger.

Nonetheless, having started it, it was not in him to quit. What he had begun he would finish, and he would hope to do enough damage in the process that they would come no more to Westwater.

It was natural that he did not consider his own situation. Not that he had not thought of it before, but he had known what his chances were, and now that he had decided to go ahead he simply would have no chance at all. At least, none worth considering.

Finally, he brought the horses out and tied them, according to plan, at the hitch-rail. He tied them with slipknots, tying Clip Hart's horse a little closer to the stable and just a little apart from the others. Then he brought the shotgun from the harness room and placed it beside the barn door, but out of sight.

He knew then he had done what he could do, and there was nothing to do but wait. He dropped into Duffy's chair and relaxed.

Word seemed to have gotten around, for no one appeared on the street. The store was open, as was the saloon, but nobody was in either place. Several times Julie came to the door and looked across the street at the young man in the chair by the barn door. Each time he was whittling. Once he even seemed to be asleep.

It was almost eleven o'clock when they heard them coming. They thundered across the bridge just outside of town and came racing around the bend and through the trees. They came at a dead run, piled off their horses and rushed for the fresh horses at the hitch-rail. Hart reached his horse and grabbed at the slipknot, and Duffy's man hit him.

There was no warning. Duffy's man had tied that horse

within an easy step and his left hook caught Hart on the chin and he went down, spun halfway around, and grabbed for his gun.

Duffy's man slapped away the gun hand and smashed Hart with a big, work-hardened fist. Knocking him back against the rail he proceeded to slug him in the belly, then on the chin with both hands. Hart went down, battered and bleeding. Only then did Duffy's man disarm him.

The other outlaws had leaped for their saddles and no sooner did they hit leather than all hell broke loose. The horses were big, fresh, and full of corn, and they began to pitch madly as if on signal. A girth broke, and then another. Men plunged into the dust, and as they hit, men rushed from the stores and ran among them, clubbing with gun barrels and rifle butts.

Duffy himself was there, moving with surprising agility for one of his age and bulk. Only one man made a break for it. He was near the stable and his cinch did not break. He got his horse turned and as he did so he lifted his pistol and took careful aim at Duffy's man.

The hostler sprang for the shotgun beside the door, knowing he would never reach it in time. Then a rifle shot rang out and as Duffy's man swung around with the shotgun in his hands, he saw the outlaw topple from his saddle into the dust.

He glanced around and saw Julie standing in the door with an old Sharps .50 in her hands, a thin wraith of smoke issuing from the muzzle.

As suddenly as that, it was over. Clip Hart was staggering to his feet, his jaw hanging and obviously broken. There was a deep cut over one eye, and his trigger finger was broken, apparently when he fell or when the gun was slapped from his hand.

One man was dead. Duffy himself had killed him when he stepped from the store. The man Julie had shot had a broken shoulder and an ugly wound where the bullet had ripped the flesh. The others had aching heads and one a broken collarbone.

Herded together in front of the livery stable, they were standing there when the posse arrived, staring at their captors who proved to be four old men, two boys of fourteen, a girl with an apron, and Duffy's man.

"They held up our bank and killed a cashier," the man with the badge told them. "If they'd gotten on those fresh horses they'd have gotten clean away. What happened?"

Duffy had been removing saddles from the horses and now he lifted a saddle blanket and lifted an ugly-looking cocklebur with blood on its stiff spines. "Somebody," he said, "put one of these under each blanket, and then cut the cinches halfway through."

The badge wearer looked at Duffy's man. "You did that?"

"Picked the meanest-looking burrs I could find. What else could I do? I'm no gunfighter!"

The sheriff looked at Hart. "Well, you're some kind of a fighter, and whatever it is, you'll do. Thanks."

Duffy looked at his holster. "Thought we was too old, did you? Well, we got fight left in us yet, ain't we, boys?"

The storekeeper gestured toward the saloon. "I'm standing for the drinks, young or old."

"Have your drink," Duffy's man said, "I'll be along soon."

He looked over at Julie. "As I said, this seemed a good place to stop."

"Are you a good man with an ax?"

"I am. But you know, it gets mighty lonely up there in the mountains. And it would help if I had somebody to cook for me, too."

"Can you cook at all?"

"No, ma'am."

"I can."

He gestured toward the church, half-hidden among the cottonwoods. "The preacher will be home tomorrow. We should make an early start."

"I will be ready." Suddenly, she was embarrassed. She dried her hands on her apron. "You go along and have that drink now."

At the saloon the men lifted their glasses to him. "Not me," he said, "I might never have done it but for something a speaker once said."

He lifted his glass. "We drink to the speaker. To Patrick Henry," he said.

"To Pat Henry," they replied.

# BIG MAN

Cherry Noble rode into Wagonstop on a black mule. He was six feet seven in his socks, and he habitually wore boots. He weighed three hundred and thirty pounds. He swung down from the mule and led it and his three pack animals to water. As he stood by the trough with his mules, the bystanders stared in unadulterated amazement.

Noble looked up, smiling in a friendly fashion. "What's off there?" He indicated the country to the west with a bob of his head.

From where he stood nothing was visible to the west but the sun setting over a weird collection of red spires and tabletopped mountains.

Lay Benton replied. "Nothin' but wilderness, some of the wildest, roughest country on earth and some bloodthirsty Indians."

"No people?"

"None."

"Water? And grass maybe?"

107

"Could be a little. Who knows?"

"Then that's where I'll go. I'll go there so when folks do come there'll be a place waiting for them. Sooner or later people come to most every place, and mostly when they get there they are hot and tired. I'll have grass, water, and beef a-waiting."

"You'd be crazy to try," Benton said. "No white man could live in that country even if the Indians would let him."

Cherry Noble's laugh boomed, his face wrinkling with the memories of old smiles. "They'll let me stay, and I guess there's no place a man can't live if he sets his mind to it." He slapped a bulging saddlebag. "Know what I've got here? Cherry pits, that's what! When I stop I plan to plant cherries! Ain't no better fruit, anywhere, and that's why people call me as they do. Noble's my name and folks call me Cherry. You could trail me across the country by the trees I've planted."

Lay Benton was a trouble-hunter, and he did not like Cherry Noble. Lay had been the biggest man around until Noble arrived, and he still considered himself the toughest. The big man's easy good humor irritated him. "If you go into that country," he said contemptuously, "you're a fool!"

" 'Better to be a fool than a knave,' " quoted Noble. He was smiling, but his eyes were measuring Benton with sudden attention and knowledge.

Benton came to his feet ready for trouble. "What was that you called me?"

Cherry Noble walked to the foot of the steps where Benton stood. "Friend"—he spoke gently, still smiling—"I didn't call you, but if you heard your name just keep a-coming."

Benton was irresolute. Something in the easy movement and confidence of the big man disturbed him. "You don't make sense!" he said irritably. "What's the matter? Are you crazy?"

Noble chuckled, his big hands on his hips. "Now as to that," he said judiciously, "there's a division of opinion. Some say yes, some say no. Me, I've not rightly decided, but at any rate I'm not a very wise man.

"Feller back in Missouri when I was about hip-high to a

short burro, he give me five books, he did. He said, 'Son, you take these books and you read them. Then you read them through again and then you ponder on 'em. After that you give them to somebody else, but there'll be something that will stay with you all the days of your life. I'm giving you the greatest gift any man can give to another.' "

Cherry Noble put one huge booted foot on the step. "Now I read them there books, and more times than twice. One was the Bible, mighty good reading whether a man is of a religious turn or not. Another was a bunch of poetry like by a man named Shakespeare. That one only made occasional sense to me until the third time around and then everything began to fall into place, and it's stayed in my mind ever since. Then there was a book on law, or that's what I was told, by Blackstone. Seemed to me that book made a lot of sense, and mostly it was rules and ideas on how folks can get along together. There was another by a man named Plato that seemed to me conversations with some other folks, but one that worried me some was an account of the death of this Socrates.

"Seems they had something against him, and the powers that were said he should take poison hemlock. Well, from the account of what happened afterward it seemed to me the man was writing about something he never actually saw because we have a sight of poison hemlock in parts of the country where I've lived and it's a very agonizing death, no way so calm and easy as this man seemed to have it.

"Man told me later, a man who was up on such things, that Plato wasn't even there when it happened. I don't think a man should write things unless he can write the truth about it, or as near as he can come to it. The other book was some sayings by Jefferson, Franklin, and the like, the sort of conclusions any reasonable man comes to in a lifetime.

"Now I read those books up one side and down the other and nothing in those books told me I was crazy and nothing in them told me I was a wise man, either. So"—he smiled cheerfully—"I just let 'er rest, an' that's a good way to do with arguments."

Noble mounted the steps and went into the store and Benton stared after him. He spat into the dust. Now what kind of a man was that?

Hack, another of the bysitters, glanced slyly at Benton. "He sure is big," he commented.

"Size doesn't make the man!" Benton said contemptuously.

The older man chuckled, looking Benton up and down. "Now that's what I've always said!" Hack agreed. "That's what I'll always say!"

The door opened and Noble stepped out. He had two one hundred pound sacks of flour under one arm and held another by the top. He walked to his pack mules and began strapping on the sacks. Then he went around to the corral and returned with three horses. Bringing out more supplies, he strapped them on the pack saddles he had brought along with the horses.

Benton had the feeling he had come out on the short end of the exchange and did not like it. Nor was he sure just how it had happened. He watched Noble loading up with growing displeasure. "Some Mormons tried to settle over there one time and the injuns run 'em out. The Green boys went in there with cattle, and the Greens were killed. You ain't got a chance back in there alone. There was six or seven of the Greens.

"Besides," he argued, "how would you make a living? Suppose your cherries grew? Where would you sell 'em?"

Cherry Noble's chuckle was rich and deep. "Why, friend, I don't worry about that. The Lord will provide, says I, and when folks come they will find the earth flowering like the gardens of paradise, with fat black cherries growing, and if by chance the injuns get me my trees will still be growing. For I say he who plants a tree is a servant of God, which I heard somewhere long ago. Even if there's no fruit on the limbs there'll be shade for the weary and a coolness in summer."

"You talk like a damned sky pilot," Benton scoffed.

"Well, I'm not one. Nor am I really what you'd call a religious man, nor a learned one. That feller who gave me the books said, 'Son, it isn't how many books you read, it's what you get from those you do read. You read those books I gave you and neither life, nor death, nor man will hold any fears for you.' That's what the man said, and he seems to have been right."

"You'll need a lot more than talk if those Piutes jump you!" Benton replied.

Noble chuckled again. "If they don't understand that kind of talk I can always use this!" He picked an empty whiskey bottle from the dust and flipped it into the air. As the bottle reached its high point he palmed his six-shooter and fired.

The shot smashed the bottle, his second and third shots broke fragments of the bottle into still smaller fragments.

Lay Benton sat down on the top step, shocked and a little sick to the stomach. To think he had been hunting trouble with a man who could shoot like that!

Noble swung into the saddle on the big mule, a huge and handsome creature who only swished his tail at the great weight. "Come visit me," he invited, "where you find me there will be green grass and trees, and if you give me time there will be black cherries ripening in the sun!"

"He'll get himself killed," Benton said sourly.

"Maybe," Hack agreed, "but injuns take to his kind."

They watched him ride down the dusty street toward the trail west, and he only stopped once, to let Ruth McGann cross in front of him. She was going over to the Border house to borrow a cup of sugar . . . at least that was what she said.

They saw that he spoke to her, and they might as well have overheard it because old man Border repeated the words.

Noble drew up and gallantly swept the hat from his head. "Beauty before industry, ma'am. You may pass before I raise a dust that might dim those lovely eyes."

She looked up at him suspiciously. "My name is Noble," he said, "and I hope that sometimes I am. They call me Cherry because it's cherries I plant wherever I've time to stop. And your name?"

"Ruth," she replied, her eyes taking in the great expanse of chest and shoulder, "and where might you be going, riding out that way?"

"Like the Hebrew children," he said, "I go into the wilderness, but I shall return. I shall come back for you, Ruth, and then you shall say to me as did Ruth of the Bible, 'Wither thou goest, I will go; and where thou lodgest, I will lodge; thy people shall be my people, and thy God, my God.' "

Ruth looked him over coolly. Seventeen and pert, she had hair like fire seen through smoke, and eyes of hazel. The prettiest girl in all that country, it was said, but with eyes for no man. "Oh, I will, will I? You've a smooth tongue, big man. What else do you have?"

"Two hands and a heart. What else will I need?"

"You'll need a head," she replied calmly. "Now be off with you. I have work to do."

"Well spoken!" He replaced his hat on his head and as Ruth passed on across the street, he added, " 'Fare you well, hereafter in a better world than this, I shall desire more love and knowledge of you.' "

Ruth McGann turned on the steps of the Border house and watched him disappear down the trail. It was only a dim trail, for not many went that way and fewer returned. "Who was that?" she asked. "I haven't seen him before."

"Some stranger," Border said, "but a mighty big man. About the biggest I ever did see."

Ruth crossed the porch and went into the house for her cup of sugar, a strange thing, as old man Border commented, for her ma had bought a barrel of sugar only a few weeks before, looking to a season's canning. The story was told around the sewing and the knitting circles for days after, and around the horse corrals and in the blacksmith shop as well. She was chided about her big man, but Ruth offered no reply.

A month passed, and then six months, and then Port Giddings came in with three riders. They had crossed the rough country to the west and stopped by the McGanns. "Wild country yonder," Port said, "but right in the midst of it we found Noble. He asked to be remembered to you, Ruth. He said to tell you when his place was in better shape he'd be coming for you."

Her eyes flashed, but she said nothing at all. Only when they talked she listened and went on with her sewing.

"The way that valley has changed you wouldn't believe," Giddings said. "He's broken sod on more than a hundred acres and has it planted to corn and oats. He's got two hundred cherry trees planted and sprouting. Then he rounded up those cattle the Green boys lost, and he's holding them on meadows thick with grass. He's using water from those old Mormon irrigation ditches, and he's cut a lot of hay.

"Best of all, he's built a stone house that's the best I've seen in this country. That man sure does work hard."

"What about the Indians?" McGann asked.

"That's the peculiar part. He seems to have no trouble at all. He located their camp when he first rode into the country, and he went in and had a long talk with the chief and some of the old men. He's never been bothered."

Cherry Noble could not have taken oath to that comment. The Indians living nearby had caused no trouble, nor had he made trouble for them. The same could not be said for passing war parties. A raiding band of Piutes had come into the country, stealing horses from the other Indians and at that very moment Noble was hunkered down behind some rocks at a water hole.

Luckily, he had glimpsed the Indians at the same time they saw him. He had reached the rocks around the water hole just in time. He shot the nearest Indian from the saddle and the rest of them went to the ground. Noble got the mule down on its side and out of rifle range. He readied his Winchester and reloaded his six-gun.

It was a long, slow, hot afternoon. There was no water nearer than fifteen miles except what lay in the water hole behind him. He knew that and so did the Piutes, only he had the water and they did not.

Sweat trickled down the big man's neck. He took a pull at his canteen and put a reassuring hand on the mule. The animal had been trained from birth for just this eventuality and lay quiet now.

They came suddenly and with a rush and Noble took his

time. He dropped one, then switched his rifle and missed a shot as they disappeared.

There were at least five Indians still out there. A buzzard soared expectantly overhead. He moved suddenly, further into the rocks and only in time. A warrior, knife in hand, dove at him from a rock and Noble threw up a hand, grasping the Indian's knife wrist and literally throwing the man to the ground near the pool.

Noble put a gun on him and the Indian looked up at him, judging his chances. "No good," Noble said. "You"—he gestured—"drink!"

The Indian hesitated. "Drink, damn you!" And the Indian did, then again.

"Now get up and get out. Tell them to leave me alone. I want no trouble, do you hear? No trouble.

"You steal even one head from me and I'll hunt you down and kill you all." How much the Indian understood he had no idea. "Now go!"

They went, wanting no more of this big man who lived alone.

Noble returned to his work. There were more trees to plant, a vegetable garden to fence, traps to be set for rabbits that were playing havoc with his crops.

Four days later, as if testing him, he found several steers driven off and tracked them to their camp. They had eaten heavily and were sleeping, doubting one lone man would attempt to pursue them.

He went into their camp on cat feet. He gathered their rifles and was taking a pistol from one of them when the man awakened. His eyes riveted on Noble's face and he started a yell, but the pistol barrel across his head stopped it.

Walking out of their camp he gathered their horses and led them to where his horse waited. Surprisingly, they were still asleep. Perhaps somewhere in their raiding they had found some whiskey, for they slept too soundly.

Picking up an armful of brush he tossed it on the fire and at the first crackle of flame they came awake. He was waiting for them with a gun in his hand.

They started to rise and he shouted, "No! You stay!"

They waited, watching him. They were tough men, and thank God, one of them was old enough to have judgment. "No trouble!" he reiterated. "I want no trouble!"

"My cow"—he gestured—"all mine! You go now. Don't come back!"

The oldest of the warriors looked up at him. "You say we come again, you kill all."

"I don't want to kill. White Stone Calf is my friend. You can be friend also."

"You say you kill. Can you kill me?"

"I can kill you. I do not wish to. I am a man who plants trees. I grow corn. If an Indian is hungry, I will feed him. If he is sick, I will try to make him well, but he harms my crops, if he attacks me or steals my cows or horses, I will kill him. Some have already died, how many must die before you understand me?"

"We will go," the Indian said. "You will give us our horses?"

"I will not. You have taken my time. I take your horses. Next time I shall take more horses. You go. If you come again, come in peace or I will follow to your village and many will die."

The following year there were two raids into the area, but they rode around the big man's land; and when the next winter was hard and the snows were heavy and icy winds prowled the canyons he rode into their village, and they watched him come.

He brought sides of beef and a sack of flour. He rode to the Indian to whom he had talked and dropped them into the snow before him. "No trouble," he said, "I am friend."

He turned and rode away, and they watched him go.


Giddings stopped again at the McGann home. "Dropped by to buy some stock from that Noble feller. Got fifty head of good beef from him. I reckon he's got at least three hundred head of young stuff, and he's kept a few cows fresh for milking."

"Did you say milking?" McGann was incredulous. "I never heard of a man milkin' a cow west of the Rockies."

"He's doing it." Giddings glanced slyly at Ruth. "He says women folks set store by milk cows. Gives 'em real butter and cream. For a woman who bakes, he says, that's a big help."

Ruth seemed not to hear, continuing with her sewing.

"His cherry trees are growing, and they look mighty nice. Long rows of them. He's put in a kitchen-garden, too. Seems he came prepared with all kinds of seed. He eats mighty good, that feller. Corn on the cob, cabbage, peas, carrots, onions, lots of other stuff. He's found a little gold, too."

It was this last item that reached the attention of Lay Benton. It was just like that crazy man, he thought, to find gold where nobody else had even looked for it. His grudge against Noble had grown as stories of his improving ranch continued to spread. He took that success as a personal affront.

Late on a night after another of Giddings' visits, Lay met with Gene Nevers and Ab Slade. "He's got gold, horses, cattle, and some cash money Giddings paid him. Must run to seven or eight hundred dollars."

"How do you figure to do it?" Slade asked.

"Take no chances. We lay for him and shoot him down. There's nobody there but him and everybody will think injuns done it."

At daylight they rode out of town, and Giddings saw them go. He stopped by the McGann house. "I shouldn't have mentioned that gold," he said. "Benton, Slade, and Nevers rode out of town, then circled and headed west."

"You think they're going after Noble?" McGann asked.

"Where else? Benton never liked him, and we all know what Benton is."

Ruth sat quietly sewing and did not look up. Giddings glanced at her. "You don't look worried," he commented.

She looked up at him. "Why should I be? If a man can't look after himself of what account is he?"

"By the way." Giddings smiled at her. "He said for you to get to work on that trousseau."

Her eyes flashed. "Does he think me a fool?"

Three days went by and there was no change in Ruth, or if there was it went unnoticed by old man Border, who missed nothing. Except, he added, that lately Ruth had been watering her flowers nine or ten times a day, and each time she took a long time shading her eyes down the trail toward the west. The trail was always empty, and the purple hills of evening told her nothing.

Benton might have been loudmouthed and Ab Slade a coward, but Gene Nevers was neither. He was an experienced outlaw and stock thief, and he had killed several men.

Benton wanted to slip up on Noble and shoot him down from ambush, but Nevers was practical. "He'll have that gold hid, and we'll never find it."

"Maybe we should catch him and burn him a little. Make him talk."

Nevers was impatient. "Don't be a fool! His kind never talks."

At the last they decided that was the way to do it. They slipped down near the house and were waiting when Noble went to the spring for water. As he straightened up his eye caught the glint of light on a rifle barrel, and he was unarmed.

He made a very big target, and he was no fool. These men had come to rob him first and then kill him. Had it been only the latter he would already be dead. He thought swiftly and coolly. The only reason he was alive was because they needed him to locate the gold.

As the three stepped into the open his eyes went from one to the other. Nevers was at once the most dangerous and the most reasonable. Slade hung back, either overly cautious or a coward. That Benton disliked him he knew.

"Howdy, gents! Why all the guns? You been hunting?"

"We were hunting you," Benton said.

"A long way to come and a big risk for what there is in it," he said.

"Where's the gold, Noble?" Nevers asked. "It will save trouble if you tell us."

"Most likely, but I never paid much mind to trouble. Kind

of liked it now and again. Keeps the edge on a man." If he could just get within reach—

He moved toward the door and instantly the guns lifted. "Hold it now!" Benton was eager to shoot.

"Just aimin' to set my bucket inside. No use to talk out here in the sun. I was just fixin' to have breakfast, so if you boys don't mind, we'll just have breakfast first and then talk. I'm hungry."

"So am I." Slade moved toward the door.

"Ab," Nevers said, "you go inside and pick up his guns. Move them into the farthest corner, behind where we will sit. We will let this man fix our breakfast, like he says. I'm hungry, too."

Ab Slade went inside and Noble knew what he was doing, he could follow his every move. He came to the door. "All right, just a Winchester and a couple of forty-fours."

They went inside. Putting down his bucket Noble went to work. He had no plan, no idea. He would fix breakfast as promised. Besides, he was hungry himself.

They stayed across the room from him, but Nevers was very alert. Several times he might have surprised the others but not Nevers.

"I found gold, all right"—he talked as he worked—"but not much of it yet. You boys came too soon. You should have waited another month or two when I'd cleaned up the sluice after some long runs. I'd just finished the sluice and now it's a loss. Too bad."

"Why too bad?" Benton asked.

"The claim will be lost. Nobody could find it but me, and after you boys kill me you'll have to skip the country. You'll never dare show face around Wagonstop again, so the gold won't do you any good."

"We ain't leavin'," Slade said. "We'll say it was injuns."

"That won't work." Noble slapped some beef in the frying pan. "I'm friends with all the Indians. In fact, they're due over here now. I promised them some beef and some tobacco."

Nevers glanced uneasily out the door. Giddings had said

that Noble was friendly with the Indians. Suppose they appeared now, and suspected something was wrong?

Noble knew what was in his mind. "You boys may have to kill your horses getting out of here because those injuns will be right after you. I've been helping them through some hard times." He forked beef from the pan. "How you figuring on getting out? Unless you know the country you're in a trap."

"Southwest," Benton said, "to Arizona."

"See? You don't know this country. The Colorado Canyon, looks like it's a mile deep, lies right in the way."

Gene Nevers swore mentally, remembering that canyon only then. He had never been south from here, only east and north. Wagonstop was east and the Indians were north. For the first time he was worried.

"You'd better get outside, Ab, and watch for those Indians."

"They're touchy," Noble said, "shoot one of them, and they'll really come after you."

He dished up the food, placing plates before Nevers and Benton. Both men had drawn their guns and placed them on the table beside their plates. Cherry Noble noted the fact and turned back to the fireplace.

Beside the woodpile was the old burlap sack in which he had the guns he had taken from the Piutes. An old blanket was partly thrown over it. In that sack there were weapons . . . but were they loaded? Could he, he asked himself, be sure of getting a loaded weapon if he dropped to one knee and grabbed? There was no certainty, and there would be no second chance.

Carefully he placed two cups on the table and picked up the coffeepot. Nevers watched him with hawk eyes as he filled the cups. Then they took their cups in their left hands and as Noble filled his own cup inspiration came. He reached for a spoon and accidentally knocked it to the floor. Stooping to retrieve it, he hurled himself against the legs of the table.

His three hundred and thirty pounds hit the table like an avalanche, smashing it back into the two outlaws. Nevers grabbed wildly at his gun and it exploded, sending a bullet into the wall as the table hit him waist-high. He was smashed backward and with Benton slammed against the wall, the boiling coffee cascading over them.

Leaping up, Noble sent a huge fist that smashed into Benton's face. His head hit the wall with a thud. Nevers pulled free of the table, gasping for breath, and lunged at Noble sending them both crashing to the floor. Nevers swung wildly, and the blow caught Noble on the chin. He might as well have hit a stone wall.

Jerking free, Nevers grabbed for his gun which lay on the floor. Nevers got a hand on the gun and Noble grabbed for Benton's gun. Nevers fired wildly and missed, then fired again and didn't. Noble felt the bullet hit him and fired in return.

He saw Nevers fall and heard running feet as Ab Slade rushed the door. He turned, swaying, and fired as Slade framed himself in the door.

Slade fell. Fully conscious, slumped against the door jamb, he said, "You got Gene?"

"Yes."

"And Benton?"

"He's out cold."

Slade stared at him, almost pleading. "I tried, didn't I? They can't say I was yella, can they?"

"You tried, Ab. You really tried. You could have run."

"Tell them that. Tell them I—" He rolled over, out of the doorway to the hard-packed earth outside.

He died like that and Cherry Noble went back inside.


On the sixth day after Benton, Slade, and Nevers rode out of town, Ruth McGann walked up the street to the store. She lingered over her shopping, listening for the news. There was none.

Then somebody in the street let out a yell. The store emptied into the street.

There was no mistaking the rider on the black mule. Behind him there were three horses. Two with empty saddles, the third with a rider tied to his horse. That rider's face was battered and swollen. Cherry Noble drew up before the store.

"They came hunting me. Two are buried back yonder. If anybody wants to collect them, they can. I caught one but not bad. Not enough to worry about. This one"—he indicated Benton—"put them up to it and as he sort of figured himself a fighter I turned him loose and let him have at it. He didn't cut much ice as a fighter."

Ruth stepped off the porch and walked away in the dust. Cherry Noble glanced after her, threw one longing look at the saloon and the beer he had wanted for the last thirty miles, and followed.

He caught her in three long strides. She had shortened hers, just a little. He was at a loss for words but finally he said, "I've come back."

"So you have," she replied coolly.

"We can be married by the preacher, and start for home in the morning. It's a long ride."

"Do you think I'm such a fool?" she burst out. "You told Giddings I should start a trousseau!"

"Was that foolish of me? Ruth, I loved you the moment I saw you and knew that for me there could be no other. Ruth, will you marry me?"

"You told him to tell me to start my trousseau!" she repeated. "Did you think me such a fool?"

"Why, I just thought—"

"You're the fool," she said. "I started it the morning after meeting you in the street."

" 'Women,' " Cherry started to quote, " 'are—' "

"For you," Ruth said sweetly, "the word has now become singular . . . so do not say 'women'!"

# THE MARSHAL OF SENTINEL

At eight o'clock Marshal Fitz Moore left his house and walked one block west to Gard's Saloon. It was already open and Fitz glimpsed Gard's swamper sweeping debris from the previous night. Crossing the street the marshal paused at the edge of the boardwalk to rub out his cigar on the top of the hitching rail. As he did so he turned his eyes but not his head, glancing swiftly up the narrow street alongside the saloon. The gray horse was gone.

Fitz Moore hesitated, considering this, estimating time and probabilities. Only then did he turn and enter the restaurant just ahead of him.

The Fred Henry gang of outlaws had been operating in this corner of the territory for more than two years, but the town of Sentinel had thus far escaped their attention. Fitz Moore, who had been marshal of Sentinel for more than half that time, had taken care to study the methods of Henry and his men. In recent raids the marshal had been slain within minutes before the raid began, or just at the moment the gang arrived.

122

A persistent pattern of operation had been established and invariably the raids had been timed to coincide with the availability of large sums of money. Such a time had come to Sentinel, as Fitz Moore had reason to know.

So, unless all his reasoning had failed, the town was marked for a raid within the next two hours. And he was marked for death.

Fitz Moore was a tall, spare man with a dark, narrow face and carefully trimmed mustache. Normally his face was still and cold, only his eyes seeming alive and aware.

As he entered the restaurant he removed his black, flat-crowned hat. His frock coat was unbuttoned offering easy access to the Smith & Wesson Russian .44. The gun was belted high and firmly on his left side just in front of his hipbone, butt to the right, holster at a slight angle.

Three men and two women sat at a long community table but only one murmured a greeting. Jack Thomas glanced up and said, "Good morning, Marshal," his tone low and friendly.

Acknowledging the greeting, the marshal seated himself at the far end of the table and accepted the cup of coffee poured by the Chinese cook.

With his mind closed to the drift of conversation from the far end of the table, he considered the situation that faced him. His days began in the same identical manner, with a survey of the town from each of the six windows of his house. This morning he had seen the gray horse tied behind Peterson's unused corral, where it would not be seen by a casual glance.

With field glasses the marshal examined the horse. It was streaked with the salt of dried sweat, evidence of hard riding. There were still some dark, damp spots indicating the horse had been ridden not long before, and the fact that it was still bridled and saddled indicated it would be ridden soon again. The brand was a Rocking R, not a local brand.

When Fitz Moore had returned to his living room he had seated himself and for an hour he read, occasionally glancing out of the window. The gray horse had not been moved in that time.

At eight when he left for breakfast the horse was still there, but by the time he had walked a block it was gone. And there lingered in the air a faint smell of dust.

Where was the horse?

Down the arroyo, of course, as it gave easy access to the forest and the mountain canyons where there was concealment and water. Taking into consideration the cool night, the sweat-streaked horse . . . not less than six miles to the point of rendezvous.

The rider of the gray had obviously been making a final check with a local source of information. To return to the rendezvous, discuss the situation and return gave him roughly two hours, perhaps a bit more. He would deal in minimums.

The marshal lighted a cigar, accepted a fresh cup of coffee and leaned back in his chair. He was a man of simple tastes and many appreciations. He knew little of cattle and less of mining, but two things he did know. He knew guns and he knew men.

He was aware of the cool gray eyes of the young woman, the only person present whom he did not know by sight. There was about her a haunting familiarity that disturbed him. He tasted his coffee and glanced out the window. Reason warned him he should be suspicious of any stranger in town at such a time, yet every instinct told him he need not be suspicious of her.

The Emporium Bank would be open in about an hour. A few minutes later Barney Gard would leave his saloon and cross the street with the receipts from Saturday and Sunday. It could be a considerable sum.

The Emporium safe would be unlocked by that time and, as they had been accepting money from ranchers and dust from miners, there would be plenty of cash on hand. In approximately one hour there would be no less than twenty thousand dollars in spendable cash within easy reach of grasping fingers and ready guns.

The Henry gang would, of course, know this. By now they were in the saddle, leaving their camp.

He did not know the name of the stranger who played poker with the Catfish Kid, but he had known the face. It had been the face of a man he had seen in Tascosa with Fred Henry, the bandit leader, some two years ago. Tied to this was the fact that the Rocking R was a brand registered to one Harvey Danuser, alias Dick Mawson, the fastest gunhand in the Henry outfit.

He was suddenly aware that a question had been directed to him. "What would you do, Marshal," Jack Thomas was asking, "if the Henry gang raided Sentinel?"

Fitz Moore glanced at the end of his cigar, then lifted his eyes to those of Jack Thomas. "I think," he said mildly, "I should have to take steps."

The marshal was not a precipitate man. Reputed to be both fast and accurate with a gun, he had yet to be proved locally. Once, not so long ago, he had killed the wrong man. He hoped never to make such a mistake again.

So far he had enforced the peace in Sentinel by shrewd judgment of character, appreciation of developing situations, and tactical moves that invariably left him in command. Authorized to employ an assistant, he had not done so. He preferred to work as he lived . . . alone.

He was, he acknowledged, but only to himself, a lonely man. If he possessed any capacity for affection or friendship it had not been obvious to the people of Sentinel. Yet this was an added strength. No one presumed to take him lightly or expect favoritism.

Long ago he had been considered a brilliant conversationalist and, in a time when a cowboy's saddlebags might carry a volume of the classics as often as Ned Buntline, he was known as a widely read man. He had been a captain in the cavalry of the United States, a colonel in a Mexican revolution, a shotgun messenger for Wells Fargo, and a division superintendent for the Butterfield Stage Line.

Naturally, he knew of the Henry gang. They had been operating for several years but only of late had they shown a tendency to shoot first and talk later. This seemed to indicate that at least one of the gang had become a ruthless killer.

Three marshals had been killed recently, each one shot in the back, an indication that a *modus operandi* had been established. First kill the marshal, then rob the town. With the marshal out of action it was unlikely resistance could be organized before the outlaws had escaped.

Fitz Moore dusted the ash from his cigar. He thought the gray horse had been standing long enough to let the sweat dry, which meant the horse had been ridden into town before daybreak. At that hour everything was closed and he had seen nobody on the street, and that seemed to indicate the rider had gone in somewhere. And that meant he not only knew where to go at that hour but that he would be welcomed.

So the Henry gang had an accomplice in Sentinel. When the rider of the gray horse left town that accomplice had undoubtedly been awake. With a raid imminent it was unlikely he would risk going back to sleep. What more likely place for him to be than right in this cafe? Here he could not only see who was around but would have a chance to judge the temper of the marshal.

Had anyone entered before he arrived? Fitz Moore knew everyone in the room except the girl with the gray eyes. She was watching him now.

Each of the others had a reason to be here at this hour. Barney Gard had opened his saloon and left it to the ministrations of his swamper. Jack Thomas directed the destinies of the livery stable. Johnny Haven, when he wasn't getting drunk and trying to tree the town, was a hardworking young cowhand and thoroughly trustworthy.

The older of the two women present was Mary Jameson, a plump and gossipy widow, the town's milliner, dressmaker, and Niagara of conversation. When she finished her breakfast she would walk three doors down the street and open her shop.

But what of the girl with the gray eyes? Her face was both delicate and strong, her hair dark and lovely, and she had an air of being to the manor born. Perhaps it was because she did possess that air, like someone from the marshal's own past, that she seemed familiar. And also, he thought reluctantly, she was just the sort of girl—

It was too late now, and there was no use thinking of it. He was not fool enough to believe there could be any such girl for him now. Not after all these years.

There was an antagonism in her eyes that he could not account for. He was accustomed to the attention of women but not antagonistic attention.

The marshal glanced thoughtfully at Johnny Haven. The young cowboy was staring sourly at his plate or devoting his attention to his coffee. Over his right temple was a swelling and a cut. This, coupled with a hangover, had left Johnny in a disgruntled mood. Last night had been the end of his monthly spree, and the swelling and the cut were evidences of the marshal's attention.

Johnny caught the marshal's glance and scowled. "You sure leave a man with a headache, Marshal. Did you have to slug me with a gun barrel?"

Fitz Moore dusted the ash from his cigar. "I didn't have an ax handle and nothing else would have been suitable for the job." He added casually, "Of course, I could have shot you."

Johnny was perfectly aware of the fact and some marshals would have done exactly that. Coming from Fitz Moore it was almost an apology.

"Is it so easy to kill men?" It was the girl with the gray eyes who spoke, her tone low and modulated but shaded with contempt.

"That depends," Fitz Moore replied with dignity, "on who is doing the shooting and the circumstances."

"I think"—and there was a flash of anger in her eyes—"that you would find it easy to kill. You might even enjoy killing. If you were capable of feeling anything at all."

The depth of feeling in her words was so obvious that, surprised, Johnny turned to look at her. Her face had gone pale, her eyes large.

The marshal's expression did not change. He knew Johnny understood, as any westerner would. Johnny Haven had himself given cause for shooting on more than one occasion. He also knew that what Marshal Fitz Moore had just said to him was more of an explanation than he had given any man. Fitz Moore had arrested Johnny Haven six times in as many months, for after every payday Johnny came to town hunting trouble. Yet Fitz Moore knew that Johnny Haven was simply a wild youngster with a lot of good stuff in him, one who simply needed taming and a sense of responsibility.

The girl's tone carried an animosity for which none of them could account, and it left them uneasy.

Barney Gard got to his feet and dropped a dollar on the table. Johnny Haven followed him out, and then the milliner. Jack Thomas loitered over his coffee.

"That Henry outfit has me worried, Marshal," he said. "You want me to get down the old scattergun, just in case?"

Fitz Moore watched Barney Gard through the window. The saloon keeper had paused on the walk to talk to Johnny Haven. Under the stubble of beard Johnny's face looked clean and strong, reminding the marshal, as it had before, of the face of another young man, scarcely older.

"It won't be necessary," Fitz Moore replied. "I'll handle them in my own way, in my own time. It's my job, you know."

"Isn't that a bit foolish? To refuse help?"

The contempt in her voice stirred him, but he revealed nothing. He nodded gravely. "I suppose it might be, ma'am, but I was hired to do the job and take the risks."

"Figured I'd offer," Thomas said, unwilling to let the matter drop. "You tell me what you figure to do, and I'll be glad to help."

"Another time." The marshal tasted his coffee again and looked directly at the girl. "You are new in Sentinel. Will you be staying long?"

"No."

"Do you have relatives here?"

"No."

He waited, but no explanation was offered. Fitz Moore was puzzled and he studied her from the corners of his eyes. There was no sound in the room but the ticking of the big, old-fashioned clock.

The girl sat very still, the delicate line of her profile bringing to him a faint, lost feeling, a nostalgia from his boyhood when such women as she rode to hounds, when there was perfume on the air, blue grass, picket fences . . .

And then he remembered.

Thomas got to his feet. He was a big, swarthy man, always untidy, a bulge of fat pushing his wide belt. "You need any help, Marshal, you just call on me."

Fitz Moore permitted himself one of his rare smiles. "If there is any trouble, Jack," he said gently, "you will be the first to know."

The clock ticked off the seconds after the door closed, and then the marshal broke the silence.

"Why have you come here? What can you do in this place?"

"All I have is here. Just a little west of here. I left the stage to hire a rig, and then I heard your name and I wanted to see what manner of man it would be who would kill his best friend."

He got to his feet. At that moment he knew better than ever what loneliness could mean.

"You judge too quickly. Each man must be judged against the canvas of his own time, his own world."

"There is only one way to judge a killer."

"Wait. Wait just a little while and you will see what I mean. And please . . . stay off the street today. If you need a rig I will see you get a responsible man." He walked to the door and paused with his hand on the knob. "He used to tell me about you. We talked often of you, and I came to feel I know you. I had hoped, before it happened, that someday we would meet. But in a different world than this.

"What will happen today I want you to see. I do not believe you lack the courage to watch what happens nor to revise your opinion if you feel you have been mistaken. Your brother, as you were advised in my letter, was killed by accident."

"But you shot him! You were in a great hurry to kill."

"I was in the midst of a gun battle. He ran up behind me."

"To help you."

"I believed him to be a hundred miles away, and in the town where we were I had no friends. It was quick. At such a time, one acts."

"Kill first," she said bitterly, "look afterward."

His features were stiff. "I am afraid that is what often happens. I am sorry."

He lifted the latch. "When you see what happens today, try to imagine how else it might be handled. If you cannot see this as I do, then before night comes you will think me even more cruel than you do now. But you may understand, and where there is understanding there is no hate."

Outside the door he paused and surveyed the street with care. Not much longer now.

Across from him was Gard's Saloon. One block down was his office and across the street from it his small home. Just a little beyond was an abandoned barn. He studied it thoughtfully, glancing again at Gard's with the bank diagonally across the street from the saloon, right past the milliner's shop.

It would happen here, upon this dusty street, between these buildings. Here men would die, and it was his mission to see that good men lived and had their peace, and the bad were kept from crime. As for himself, he was expendable . . . but which was he, the good or the bad?

Fitz Moore knew every alley, every door, every corner in this heat-baked, alkali-stamped cluster of life that would soon become an arena. His eyes turned again to the barn. It projected several feet beyond the otherwise carefully lined buildings. The big door through which hay had once been hoisted gaped wide.

So little time!

He knew what they said about him. "Ain't got a friend in town," he had overheard Mrs. Jameson say. "Lives to hisself in that old house. Got it full of books, folks say. But kill you quick as a wink, he would. He's cold . . . mighty cold."

Was he?

When first he came to the town he found it a shambles, wrecked by a passing trail-herd crew. It had been terrorized by two dozen gamblers and gunmen, citizens robbed by cardsharps and thieves. Robbery had been the order of the day and murder all too frequent. Now it had been six months since the last murder. Did that count for nothing?

He took out a fresh cigar and bit off the end. What was the matter with him today? He had not felt like this in years. Was it what they say happens to a drowning man and his whole life was passing before his eyes, just before the end? Or was it simply that he had seen Julia Heath, the sum and total of all he had ever wanted in a girl? And realizing who she was, realized also how impossible it had become?

They had talked of it, he and Tom Heath, and Tom had written to Julia, suggesting she come west because he had found the man for her. And two weeks later Tom was dead with his, with Fitz Moore's, bullet in his heart.

The marshal walked along the street of false-fronted, weather-beaten buildings. Squalid and dismal as they might seem to a stranger they were the center of the world for those who lived in the country around. Here where mountains and desert met, the town was changing. It was growing with the hopes of its citizens and with the changing of times and needs. This spring, for example, flowers had been planted in the yard of a house near the church, and trees had been trimmed in another.

From a haphazard collection of buildings catering to the needs of a transient people, the town of Sentinel was acquiring a sense of belonging, a consciousness of the future. The days of cattle drives were soon to be gone and where they had walked men would build and plant and harvest.

Fitz Moore turned into the empty alley between the Emporium and the general store. Thoughts of his problem returned. With the marshal dead the town would be helpless until men could gather, choose a leader, and act. For the moment the town would be helpless.

But how did they plan to kill him? That it had been planned he was sure, but it must be done soon and quickly, for the marshal would be the focal point of resistance.

The loft of the abandoned barn commanded a view of the street. The outlaws would come into town riding toward the barn and somewhere along that street the marshal of Sentinel would be walking, covered by a hidden rifleman.

He climbed up the stairs to the barn loft. The dust on the steps had been disturbed. At the top a board creaked under his boot. A rat scurried away. The loft was wide and empty, only dust and wisps of hay, a few cobwebs.

From that wide door the raid might be stopped, but this was

not the place for him. His place was down there in that hot, dusty street where his presence would count. Much remained to be done and there was but little time.

Returning to his quarters, Fitz Moore thrust an extra gun into his pocket and belted on a third. Then he put two shotguns into a wool sack. Nobody would be surprised to see him carrying the sack, for he used it to bring firewood from the pile back of Gard's.

Jack Thomas was seated in a chair in front of the livery stable. Barney Gard came from the saloon, glanced at the marshal as if to assure himself of his presence, then went back inside. Fitz Moore paused, relighting his dead cigar, surveying the street over the match and under the brim of his hat.

The topic of what might happen here if the Henry gang attempted to raid was not a new one. There had been much speculation. Several men aside from Thomas had brought up the subject, trying to feel him out, to discover what he thought, what he might plan to do.

Jack Thomas turned his head to watch the marshal. He was a big, easygoing man with a ready smile. He had been one of the first to offer his services.

Johnny Haven, seated on the steps of the saloon's porch, looked up at the marshal, grinning. "How's the town clown?" he asked.

Moore paused beside him, drawing deep on the cigar and permitting himself a glance toward the loft door, almost sixty yards away and across the street. Deliberately, he had placed himself in line with the best shooting position.

"Johnny," he said, "if anything happens to me, I want you to have this job. If nothing happens to me I want you for my deputy."

Young Haven could not have been more astonished, but he was also deeply moved. He looked up at the marshal as if he thought his mind had been affected by the heat. Aside from the words the very fact that the marshal had ventured a personal remark was astonishing.

"You're twenty-six, Johnny, and it's time you grew up. You've played at being the town roughneck long enough. I've looked the town over, and I've decided you're the man for the job."

Johnny . . . Tom. He tried to avoid thinking of them together but there was a connection. Tom had been a good man, too. Now he was a good man gone. Johnny was a good one, no question about it. He had heard many stories of how dependable he was out on the range, but Johnny was walking the hairline of the law. A step too far and he could become an outlaw.

Johnny Haven was profoundly impressed. To say that he both respected and admired this tall, composed man was no more than the truth. After Moore arrested him the first time Johnny had been furious enough to kill him, but each time he came into town he found himself neatly boxed and helpless.

Nor had Moore ever taken unfair advantage, never striking one blow more than essential, never keeping the cowhand in jail an hour longer than necessary. And Johnny Haven was honest enough to realize he could never have handled the situation as well.

Anger had dissolved into reluctant admiration. Only stubbornness and the pride of youth had prevented him from giving up the struggle.

"Why pick on me?" He spoke roughly to cover his emotion. "You won't be quitting."

There was a faint suggestion of movement from the loft. The marshal glanced at his watch. Two minutes to ten.

"Johnny—?" The sudden change of tone brought Johnny's head up sharply. "When the shooting starts there are two shotguns in this sack. Get behind the water trough and use one of them. Shoot from under the trough, it's safer."

Two riders walked their horses into the upper end of the street, almost a block away. Two men on powerful horses, much better horses than were usually found on any cow ranch.

Three more riders emerged from the space between the buildings, coming from the direction of Peterson's corral. One of them was riding a gray horse. They were within twenty yards when Barney Gard came from his saloon carrying two canvas bags. He was starting for the bank, and one of the riders reined his horse around to come between Gard and his goal.

"Shotgun in the sack, Gard." The marshal's tone was conversational.

Then, sunlight glinted on a rifle barrel in the loft door. Fitz Moore took one step forward and drew. The thunder of the rifle merged a little late with the bark of his own gun. The rifle clattered, falling, and an arm fell loosely from the loft door.

The marshal's turn was abrupt, yet smooth. "All right, Henry!" His voice like the blare of a trumpet in the narrow street. "You've asked for it! Now *take* it!"

There was no request for surrender. The rope awaited these men, death rode their hands and their guns.

As one man they went for their guns. The marshal leaped into the street, landing flat-footed and firing. The instant of surprise was his, and they were mounted on nervous horses. His first shot had killed the man in the loft, the second killed Fred Henry.

Behind and to his right a shotgun's deep roar blasted the sun-filled morning. The man on the gray horse died falling, his gun throwing a useless shot into the hot, still air.

A rider leaped his horse at the marshal but Fitz Moore stood his ground and fired. The rider's face seemed to disintegrate under the impact of the bullet.

And then there was silence. The roaring of guns was gone and only the faint smells lingered, the acrid tang of gunpowder, of blood in the dust, the brighter crimson of blood on a saddle.

Johnny Haven got up slowly from behind the horse trough. Barney Gard stared around as if just awakened, the canvas bags at his feet, his hands gripping the shotgun Johnny had thrown him.

There was a babble of sound then and people running into the street, and a girl with gray eyes watching. Those eyes seemed to reach across the street and into the heart of the marshal.

"Only one shot!" Barney Gard exclaimed. "I got off only one shot and missed that one!"

"The Henry gang wiped out!" yelled an excited citizen. "Wait until Thomas hears that!"

"He won't be listenin'," somebody said. "They got him."

Fitz Moore turned like a duelist. "I got him," he said flatly. "He was their man. He tried all morning to find out what I'd do if they showed up. Besides, he was hostler at the livery stable at the time of the holdup at the Springs."

An hour later Johnny Haven followed the marshal into the street. Four men were dead, two were in jail.

"How did you know, Marshal?"

"You learn, Johnny. You learn or you die. That's your lesson for today. Learn to be in the right place at the right time and keep your own counsel. You'll be getting my job." His cigar was gone. He bit the end from another and continued.

"Jack Thomas was the only man the rider of the gray horse could have visited without crossing the street. No outlaw would have left the horse he would need for a quick getaway on the wrong side of the street."

When he returned to the eating house Julia Heath was at her table again. She was white and shaken.

"I am sorry, Julia, but now you know how little time there is when guns are drawn. These men came to steal the money honest men worked to earn, and they would have killed again as they have killed before. Such men know only the law of the gun." He placed his hands on the table. "I should have recognized you at once, Julia, but I never imagined, after what happened, that you would come. I had forgotten about Tom's ranch. He was proud of you, Julia, and he was my best friend."

"But you killed him."

Marshal Moore gestured toward the street. "It was like that. Guns exploding, a man dying almost at my feet, then someone rushing up behind me in a town where I had no friends. I fired at a man who was shooting at me, turned and fired at one running up behind me. I killed my best friend, your brother."

She knew now how it must have been for this man, and she was silent.

"And now?" she asked finally.

"My job goes to Johnny Haven, but I shall stay here and try

to help the town grow. This fight should end it for a while. In the meantime the town can mature, settle down, and become a place to live in instead of just a place to camp for the night."

"I—I guess it's worth doing."

"It is." He put down his unlighted cigar. "You will be driving over to settle Tom's estate. When you come back you might feel like stopping off again. If you do, I'll be waiting to see you."

She looked at him, looking beyond the coldness, the stillness, seeing the man her brother must have known. "I think I shall. I think I will stop . . . when I come back."

Out in the street a man was raking dust over the blood. Back of the barn an old hen cackled, and somewhere a pump began to complain rustily, drawing clear water from a deep, cold well.

# BLUFF CREEK STATION

The stage was two hours late into Bluff Creek and the station hostler had recovered his pain-wracked consciousness three times. After two futile attempts to move himself he had given up and lay sprawled on the rough boards of the floor with a broken back and an ugly hole in his side.

He was a man of middle years, his jaw unshaved and his hair rumpled and streaked with gray. His soiled shirt and home-spun jeans were dark with blood. There was one unlaced boot on his left foot. The other boot lay near a fireplace gray with ancient ashes.

There were two benches and a few scattered tools, some odd bits of harness, an overturned chair, and a table on which were some unwashed dishes. Near the hostler's right hand lay a Spencer rifle, and beyond it a double-barreled shotgun. On the floor nearby, within easy reach, a double row of neatly spaced shotgun and rifle shells. Scattered about were a number of used shells from both weapons, mute mementos of his four-hour battle with attacking Indians.

Now, for slightly more than two hours there had been no attack, yet he knew they were out there, awaiting the arrival of the stage, and it was for this he lived, to fire a warning shot before the stage could stop at the station. The last shot they fired, from a Sharps .50, had wrecked his spine. The bloody wound in his side had come earlier in the battle, and he had stuffed it with cotton torn from an old mattress.

Outside, gray clouds hung low, threatening rain, and occasional gusts of wind rattled the dried leaves on the trees, or stirred them along the hard ground.

The stage station squatted in dwarfish discomfort at the foot of a bluff, the station was constructed of blocks picked from the slide-rock at the foot of the bluff, and it was roofed with split cedar logs covered with earth. Two small windows stared in mute wonderment at the empty road and at the ragged brush before it where the Indians waited.

Three Indians, he believed, had died in the battle, and probably he had wounded as many more, but he distrusted counting Indian casualties, for all too often they were overestimated. And the Indians always carried away their dead.

The Indians wanted the stage, the horses that drew it, and the weapons of the people inside. There was no way to warn the driver or passengers unless he could do it. The hostler lay on his back staring up at the ceiling.

He had no family, and he was glad of that now. Ruby had run off with a tinhorn from Alta some years back, and there had been no word from her, nor had he wished for it. Occasionally, he thought of her, but without animosity. He was not, he reminded himself, an easy man with whom to live, nor was he much of a person. He had been a simple, hardworking man, inclined to drink too much, and often quarrelsome when drinking.

He had no illusions. He knew he was finished. The heavy lead slug that had smashed the base of his spine had killed him. Only an iron will had kept life in his body, and he doubted his ability to keep it there much longer. His legs were already dead and there was a coldness in his fingers that frightened him. He would need those fingers to fire the warning shot.

Slowly, carefully, he reached for the shotgun and loaded it with fumbling, clumsy fingers. Then he wedged the shotgun into place in the underpinning of his bunk. It was aimed at nothing, but all he needed was the shot, the dull boom it would make, a warning to those who rode the stage that something was amiss.

He managed to knot a string to the trigger so it could be pulled even if he could not reach the trigger. His extremities would go first and then even if his fingers were useless he could pull the trigger with his teeth.

Exhausted by his efforts he lay back and stared up at the darkening ceiling, without bitterness, waiting for the high, piercing yell of the stage driver and the rumble and rattle of the stage's wheels as it approached the station.

Five miles east, the heavily loaded stage rolled along the dusty trail accompanied by its following plume of dust. The humped-up clouds hung low over the serrated ridges. Up on the box, Kickapoo Jackson handled the lines and beside him Hank Wells was riding shotgun. Wells was deadheading it home as there was nothing to guard coming west. He had his revolving shotgun and a rifle with him from force of habit. The third man who rode the top, lying between some sacks of mail, was Marshal Brad Delaney, a former buffalo hunter and Indian fighter.

Inside the stage a stocky, handsome boy with brown hair sat beside a pretty girl in rumpled finery. Both looked tired and were, but the fact that they were recently married was written all over them. Half the way from Kansas City they had talked of their hopes and dreams, and their excitement had been infectious. They had enlisted the advice and sympathy of those atop the coach as well as those who rode inside.

The tall man of forty with hair already gray at the temples was Dr. Dave Moody, heading for the mining camps of Nevada to begin a new practice after several years of successful work in New England. Major Glen Faraday sat beside him at the window. Faraday was a West Point man, now discharged from the army and en route west to build a flume for an irrigation project.

Ma Harrigan, who ran a boardinghouse in Austin and was reputed to make the best pies west of the Rockies, sat beside Johnny Ryan, headed west to the father he had never seen.

Kickapoo Jackson swung the Concord around a bend and headed into a narrow draw. "Never liked this place!" he shouted. "Too handy for injuns!"

"Seen any around?" Delaney asked.

"Nope! But the hostler at Bluff Creek had him a brush with them awhile back. He driv 'em off, though! That's a good man, yonder!"

"That's his kid down below," Wells said. "Does he know the kid's comin' west?"

"Know?" Kickapoo spat. "Ryan don't even know he's got a kid! His wife run off with a no-account gambler a few years back! When the gambler found she was carryin' another man's child he just up and left her. She hadn't known about the kid when she left Ryan."

"She never went back?"

"Too proud, I reckon. She waited tables in Kansas City awhile, then got sickly. Reckon she died. The folks the boy lived with asked me to bring him back to his dad. Ol' Ryan will sure be surprised!"

The grade steepened and Jackson slowed the stage for the long climb. Brad Delaney sat up and surveyed the sage-covered hills with a wary eye, cradling his Winchester on his knees. No chance of surprising them here despite their slow pace. Here the Indians would be in the open which would mean suicide for them. Hank Wells was a seasoned fighting man and there wasn't a better man with the ribbons than old Kickapoo.

Down inside they had Doc, who had fought in the war between the states, and the major, who was a veteran soldier. The newly married kid handled a rifle like he knew what it was meant for, and unless they were completely surprised, any batch of raiders would run into trouble with this stage.

At Bluff Creek all was quiet. Dud Ryan stared up into the gathering darkness and waited. From time to time he could put an eye to a crack and study the road and the area beyond it. They were there . . . waiting.

Delaney and Wells would be riding the stage this trip, and they were canny men. Yet they would not be expecting trouble at the stage station. When they rolled into sight of it there would be a letdown, an easing-off, and the Indians would get off a volley before the men on the stage knew what hit them.

With Brad and Hank out of the picture, and possibly Kickapoo Jackson, the passengers could be slaughtered like so many mice. Caught inside the suddenly stalled stage, with only its flimsy sides to protect them, they would have no chance.

Only one thing remained. He must somehow remain alive to warn them. A warning shot would have them instantly alert, and Hank Wells would whip up his team and they would go through and past the station at a dead run. To warn them he must be alive.

Alive?

Well, he knew he was dying. He had known from the moment he took that large caliber bullet in the spine. Without rancor he turned the idea over in his mind. Life hadn't given him much, after all. Yet dying wouldn't be so bad if he felt that his dying would do any good.

The trouble was, no man was ever ready to die. There was always something more to do, something undone, even if only to cross the street.

Behind him the years stretched empty and alone. Even the good years with Ruby looked bleak when he thought of them. He had never been able to give her anything, and maybe that was why he drank. Like all kids he had his share of dreams, and he was ready to take the world by the throat and shake it until it gave him the things he desired. Only stronger, more able men seemed always to get what he wanted. Their women had the good things and there had been nothing much he could do for Ruby. Nor much for himself but hard work and privation.

At that, Ruby had stuck by him even after he began to hit the bottle too hard. She used to talk of having a nice house somewhere, and maybe of traveling, seeing the world and meeting people. All he had given her was a series of small mining camps, ramshackle cabins, and nothing much to look forward to but more of the same. His dream, like so many others, was to make the big strike, but he never had.

The tinhorn was a slick talker and Ruby was pretty, prettier than most. He had talked mighty big of the places he would show her, and what they would do. Even when Dud followed him home one night and gave him a beating, Ruby had continued to meet him. Then they ran off.

At the time they had been just breaking even on what he made from odd jobs, and then he got a steady job with the stage line. He rushed home with the news, for it meant he'd have charge of the station at Haver Hill, a cool, pleasant little house where they could raise some chickens and have a flower garden as well as a place to raise garden truck. It was always given to a married man, and he had landed it. He rushed home with the news.

The house was empty. He had never seen it so empty because her clothes were gone and there was only the note . . . he still had it . . . telling him she was leaving him.

He gave up Haver Hill then and took a series of bad stations where the work was hard and there was much fighting. His salary wasn't bad and he had saved some money, bought a few horses, and broke teams during his spare time. The stage company itself had bought horses from him, and he was doing well. For the first time he managed to save some money, to get ahead.

There was no word from Ruby although he never stopped hoping she would write. He did not want her back, but he hoped she was doing well and was happy. Also, he wanted her to know how well he was doing.

He did hear about the tinhorn, and it was from Brad Delaney that he got the news. The tinhorn had showed up in El Paso alone. From there he drifted north to Mobeetie, and finally to Fort Griffin. There he had tried to outsmart a man who was smarter, and when caught cheating he tried to outdraw him.

"What happened?" Dud had asked.

"What could happen? He tackled a man who wouldn't take anything from anybody, some fellow who used to be a dentist but was dying of tuberculosis. That dentist put two bullets into that tinhorn's skull, and he's buried in an unmarked grave in Boot Hill."

Dud Ryan wrote to El Paso but the letter was returned. There was no trace of Ruby. Nobody knew where the tinhorn had come from and the trail ended there. Ryan had about convinced himself that Ruby was dead.

He tried to move, but the agony in his back held him still. If only he could live long enough! Where the hell was the stage? It should have been along hours ago.

He ground his teeth in pain and set his mind on the one thought: *Live! Live! Live!*

Delaney, Wells, and old Kickapoo were too good to die in an ambush. They were strong men, decent men, the kind the country needed. They wouldn't have let him down, and he'd be damned if he would fail them.

I'm tough, he told himself, I'm tough enough to last.

He tried and after a moment succeeded in lifting his hand. His fingers were clumsy and his hand felt cold. There were no Indians in sight, but he dared not fire, anyway, for he could never load the gun again. He just had to wait . . . somehow.

He could no longer make out the split logs in the ceiling. The shadows were darker now, and the room was darker. Was it really that much later? Or was he dying? Was this part of it?

Once he thought he heard a far off yell, and he gripped the triggers of the shotgun, but the yell was not repeated. His lips fumbled for words, fumbled through the thickening fog in his brain. *Live!* he told himself. You've got to *live!*

"Ruby," he muttered, " 's all right, Ruby. I don't blame you."

He worked his mouth but his lips were dry, and his tongue felt heavy in his mouth. "Live!" he whispered. "Please, God! Let me live!"

Something stirred in the brush across the way, and the shadow of movement caught his eye. An Indian was peering toward the station. And then wild and clear he heard Kickapoo's yell. "*Yeeow!*"

Dud Ryan felt a fierce surge of joy. He'd made it! By the

Lord Harry, he'd—! He tried to squeeze, but his fingers failed him and his hand fell away, fell to the floor.

He could hear the pound of hooves now, and the rattle of the stage.

He rolled over, the stabbing pain from his broken spine wrenching a scream from him, but in a last, terrible burst of energy he managed to grasp the rawhide in his teeth and jerk down. The twin barrels of the shotgun thundered, an enormous bellow of sound in the empty room. Instantly there was a crash of sound, the rolling stage, rifles firing, and all hell breaking loose outside.

Kickapoo Jackson was rolling the stage down the slight hill to Bluff Creek when he heard the roar of the gun. Brad Delaney came up on his knees, rifle in hand, but it was Wells with the revolving shotgun who saw the first Indian. His shotgun bellowed and Delaney's rifle beat out a rapid tattoo of sound, and from below pistols and a rifle were firing.

The attack began and ended in that brief instant of gunfire, for the Indians were no fools and their ambush had failed. Swiftly, they retired, slipping away in the gathering darkness and carrying three dead warriors with them.

Jackson sawed the team to a halt, and Delaney dropped to the ground and sent three fast shots after the retreating Indians.

Doc Moody pushed open the door and saw the dying man, the rawhide still gripped in his teeth. With a gentle hand he took it away.

"You don't need to tell me, Doc. I've had it." Sweat beaded his forehead. "I've known for . . . hours. Had—had to . . . warn. . . ."

Hank Wells dropped to his knees beside Ryan. "Dud, you saved us all, but you saved more than you know. You saved your own son!"

"Son?"

"Ruby had a boy, Dud. Your boy. He's four now, and he's outside there with Ma Harrigan."

"My boy? I saved my boy?"

"Ruby's dead, Ryan," Delaney said. "She was sending the boy to you, but we'll care for him, all of us."

He seemed to hear, tried to speak, and died there on the floor at Bluff Creek Station.

Doc Moody got to his feet. "By rights," he said, "that man should have been dead hours ago."

"Guts," Hank Wells said, "Dud never had much but he always had guts."

Doc Moody nodded. "I don't know how you boys feel about it, but I'm adopting a boy."

"He'll have four uncles then," Jackson said. "The boy will have to have a family."

"Count us in on that," the newlywed said. "We want to be something to him. Maybe a brother and sister, or something."

They've built a motel where the stage station stood, and not long ago a grandson and a great-grandson of Dud Ryan walked up the hill where some cedar grew, and stood beside Dud Ryan's grave. They stopped only a few minutes, en route to a family reunion.

There were fifty-nine descendants of Dud Ryan, although the name was different. One died in the Argonne Forest and two on a beach in Normandy and another died in a hospital in Vietnam after surviving an ambush. There were eleven physicians and surgeons at the reunion, one ex-governor, two state senators, a locomotive engineer, and a crossing guard. There were two bus drivers and a schoolteacher, several housewives, and a country storekeeper. They had one thing in common: They all carried the blood of Ryan, who died at Bluff Creek Station on a late October evening.